THE
WIND IN THE
WILLOWS

KENNETH GRAHAME

CAMPFIRE™

KALYANI NAVYUG MEDIA PVT. LTD
New Delhi

Sitting around the Campfire, telling the story, were:

Wordsmith	:	Arjun Gaind
Author	:	Kenneth Grahame
Illustrator	:	Sankha Banerjee
Colorist	:	Prasanth K. G.
Colorist (Information Pages)	:	Vijay Sharma
Letterers	:	Laxmi Chand Gupta Bhavnath Chaudhary
Editors	:	Divya Dubey Aditi Ray
Editor (Informative content)	:	Jayshree Das
Production Controller	:	Vishal Sharma

Cover Artists:

Illustrator	:	Sankha Banerjee
Colorist	:	Pradeep Sherawat
Designer	:	Jayakrishnan K. P.

Published by Kalyani Navyug Media Pvt. Ltd
101 C, Shiv House, Hari Nagar Ashram
New Delhi 110014
India
www.campfire.co.in

ISBN: 978-93-80028-54-5

Printed in India at Rave India

About the Author

Kenneth Grahame was born in Edinburgh in 1859. He spent his childhood in the Western Highlands of Scotland, but after the death of his parents, was sent to live with his grandmother in Berkshire. It was her house and garden on the bank of the river Thames that would later provide the inspiration for his opus, *The Wind in the Willows*.

Written in 1908 for Grahame's partially blind son, Alistair (nicknamed Mouse), *The Wind in the Willows* is a charming evocation of the idyllic world of a rural riverbank, untouched by the smoke, smog, and squalor of the Industrial Age.

Although the original book wasn't an immediate success when it was first published in 1929, *The Wind in the Willows* was adapted by A. A. Milne as a musical entitled *Toad of Toad Hall*, and thus rescued from obscurity. Since then, it has gone on to become one of the most treasured classics of children's literature. It remains to this day a charming testament to a bygone age of simplicity and innocence that has long since been lost.

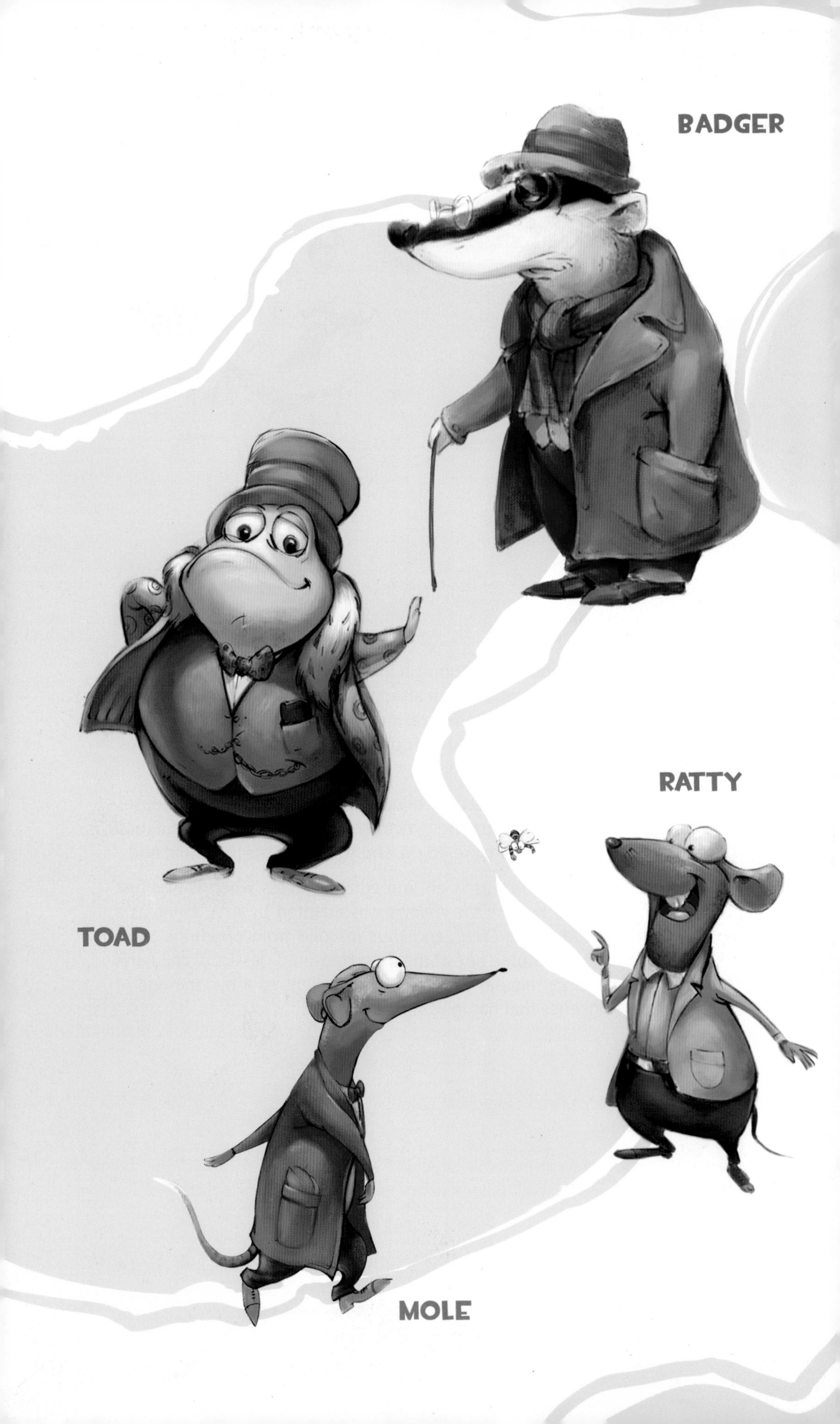
BADGER
RATTY
TOAD
MOLE

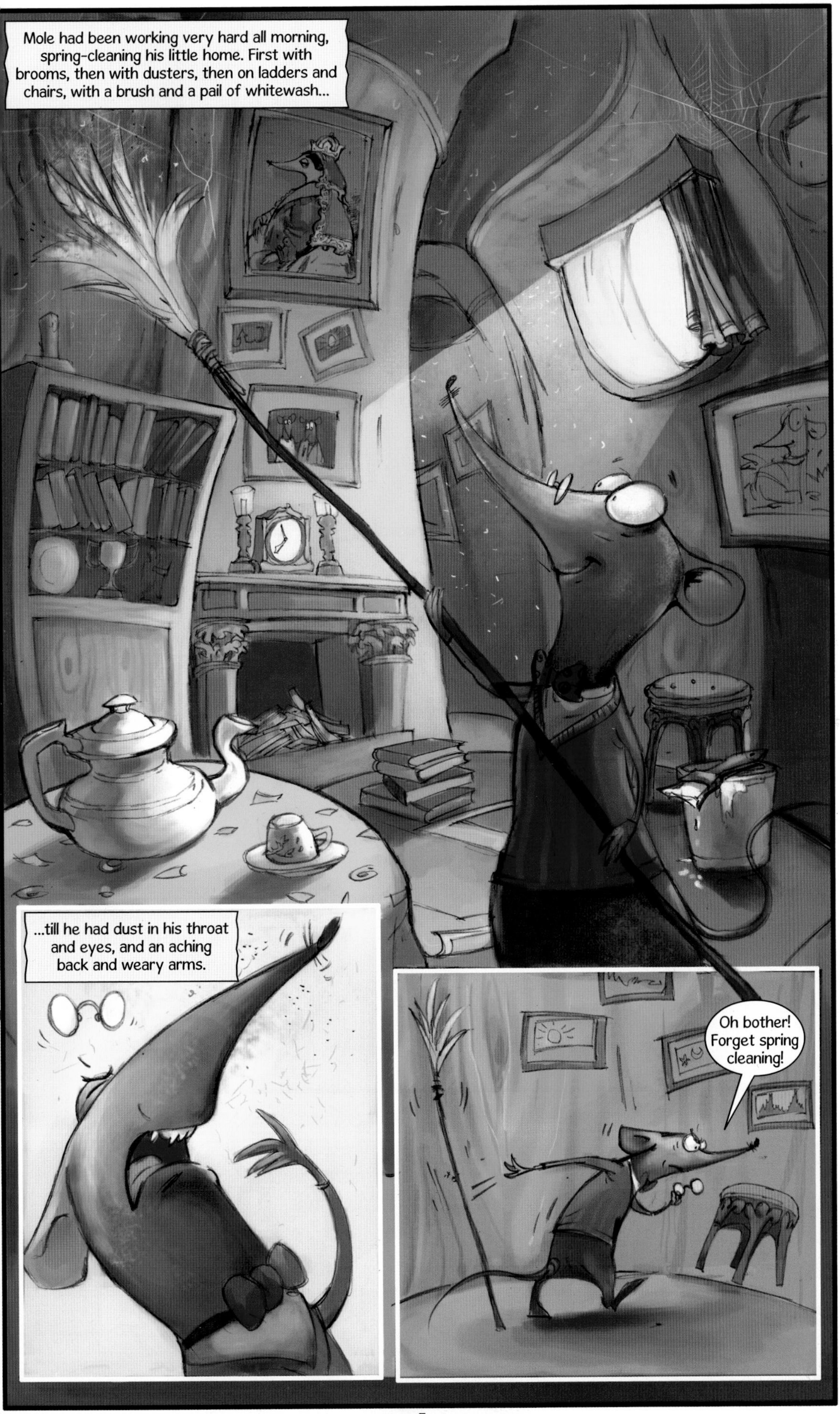
Mole had been working very hard all morning, spring-cleaning his little home. First with brooms, then with dusters, then on ladders and chairs, with a brush and a pail of whitewash...
...till he had dust in his throat and eyes, and an aching back and weary arms.
Oh bother! Forget spring cleaning!

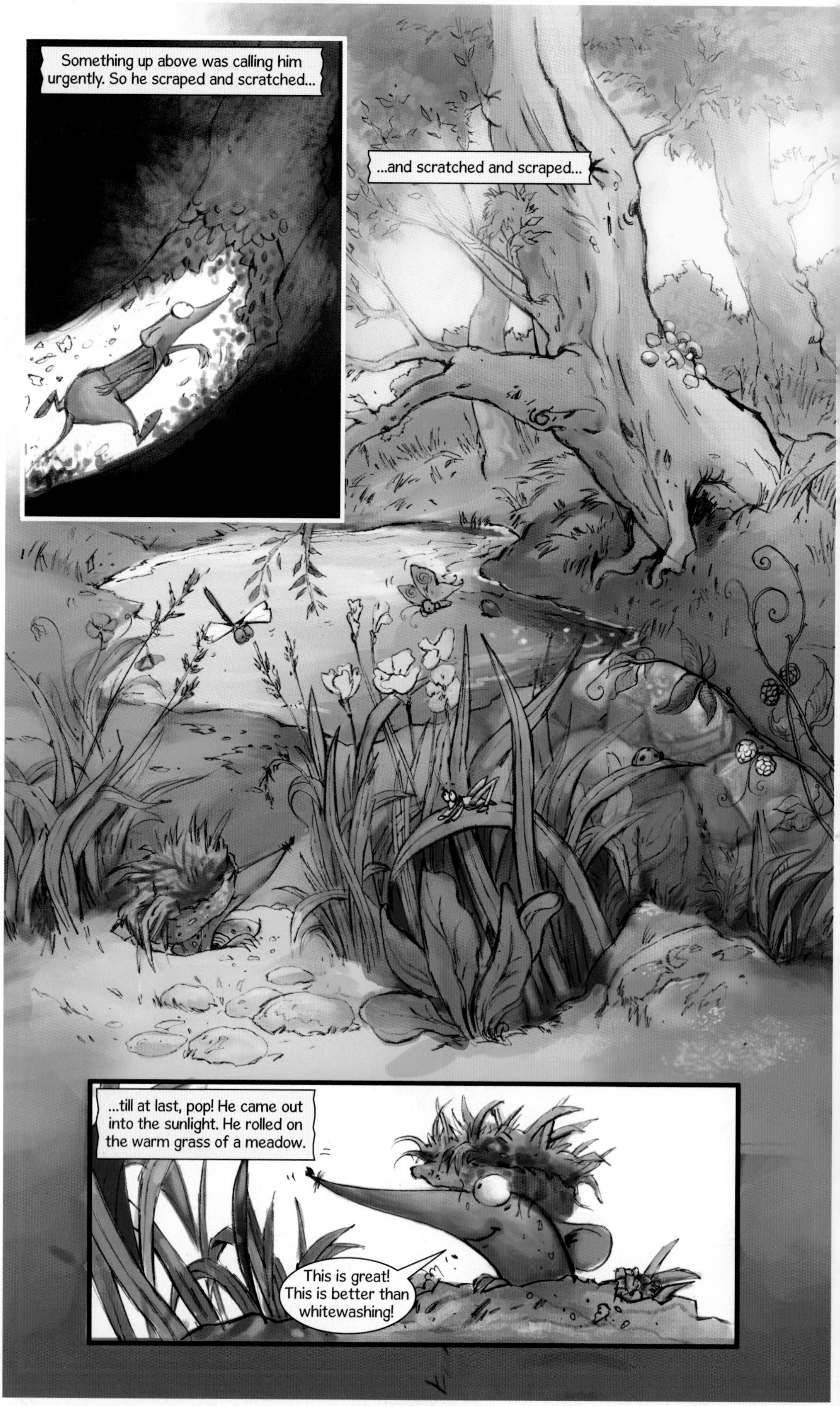
Something up above was calling him urgently. So he scraped and scratched...
...and scratched and scraped...
...till at last, pop! He came out into the sunlight. He rolled on the warm grass of a meadow.
This is great! This is better than whitewashing!

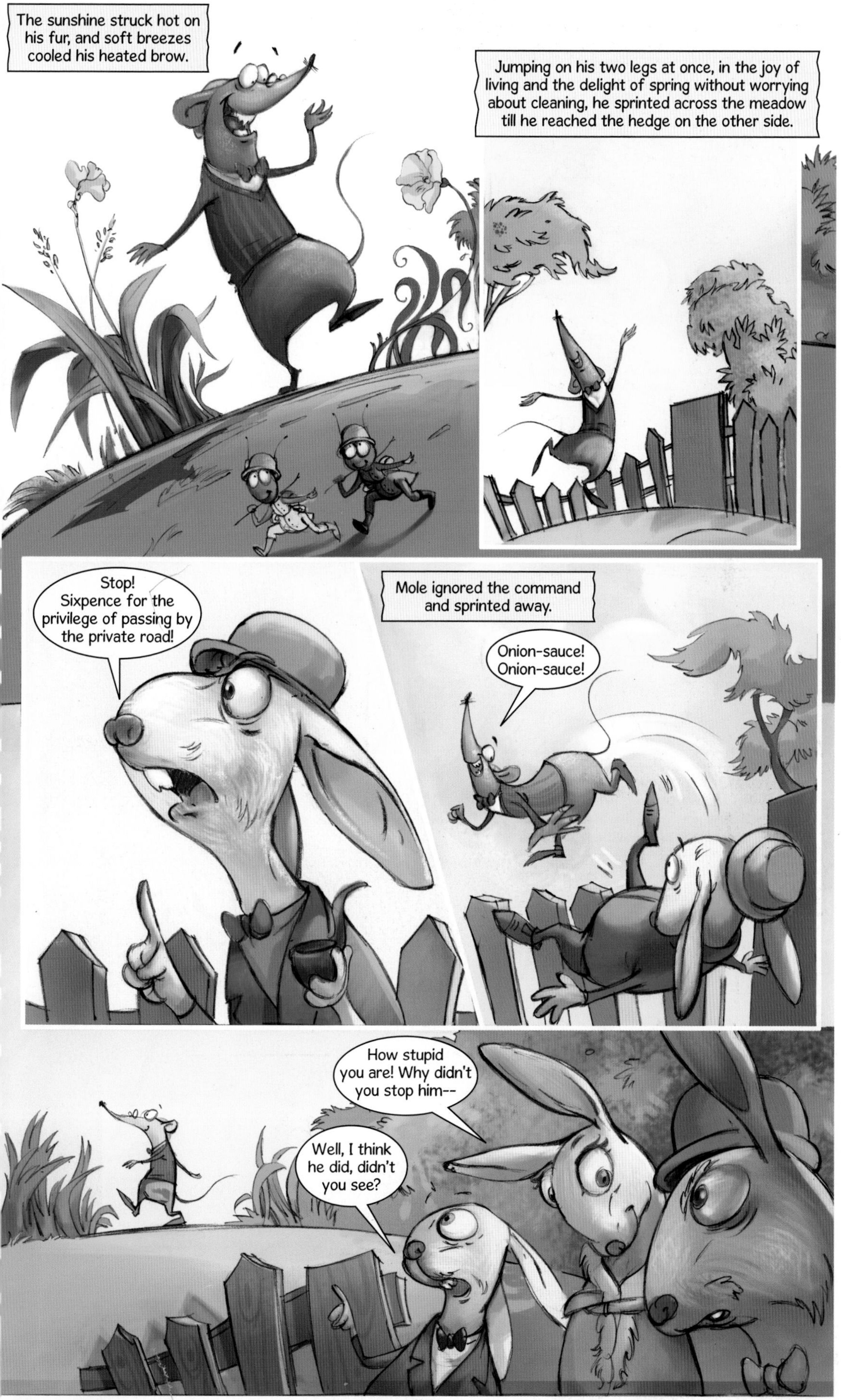
The sunshine struck hot on his fur, and soft breezes cooled his heated brow.
Jumping on his two legs at once, in the joy of living and the delight of spring without worrying about cleaning, he sprinted across the meadow till he reached the hedge on the other side.
Stop! Sixpence for the privilege of passing by the private road!
Mole ignored the command and sprinted away.
Onion-sauce! Onion-sauce!
How stupid you are! Why didn't you stop him--
Well, I think he did, didn't you see?

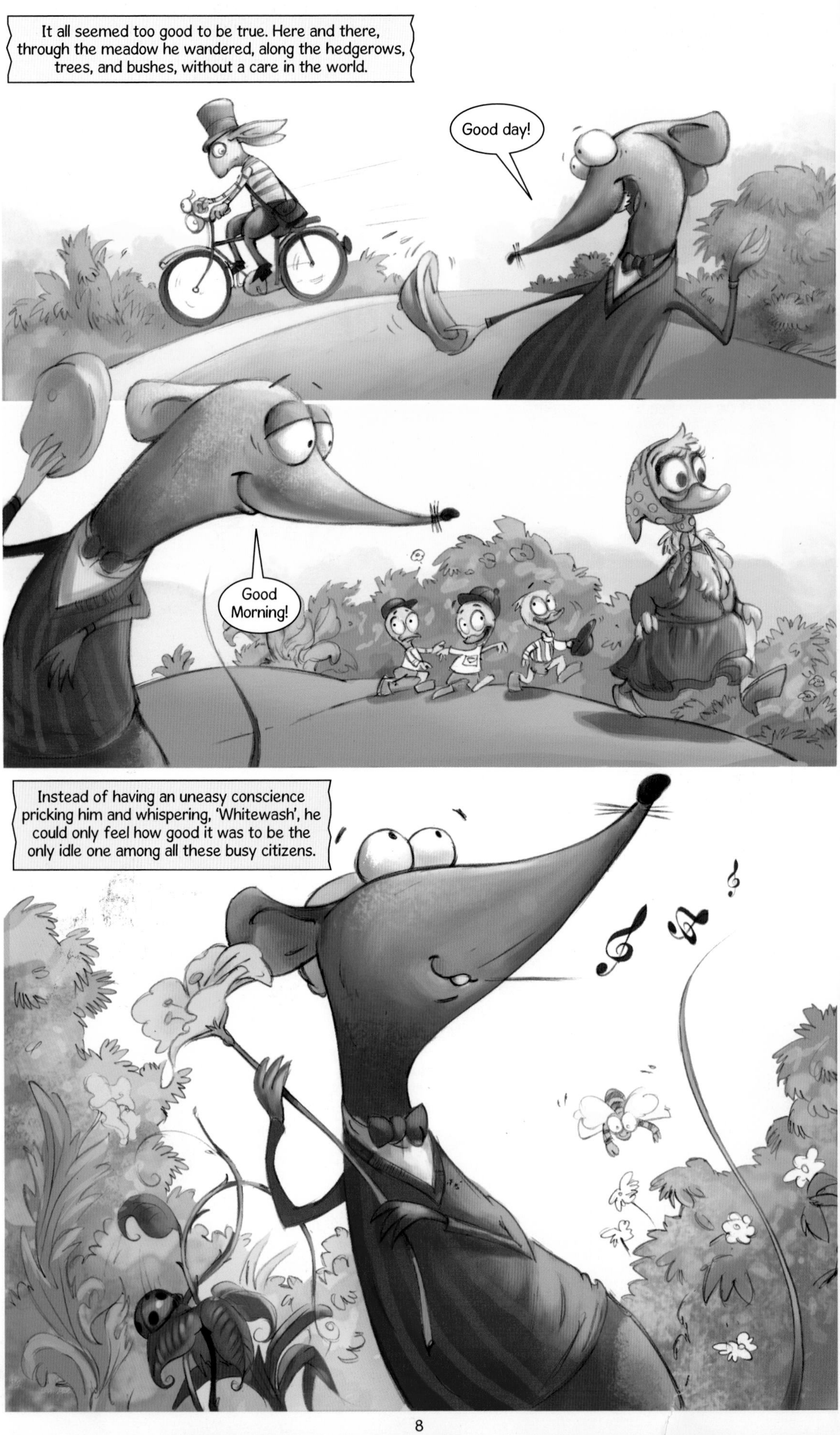
It all seemed too good to be true. Here and there, through the meadow he wandered, along the hedgerows, trees, and bushes, without a care in the world.
Good day!
Good Morning!
Instead of having an uneasy conscience pricking him and whispering, 'Whitewash', he could only feel how good it was to be the only idle one among all these busy citizens.

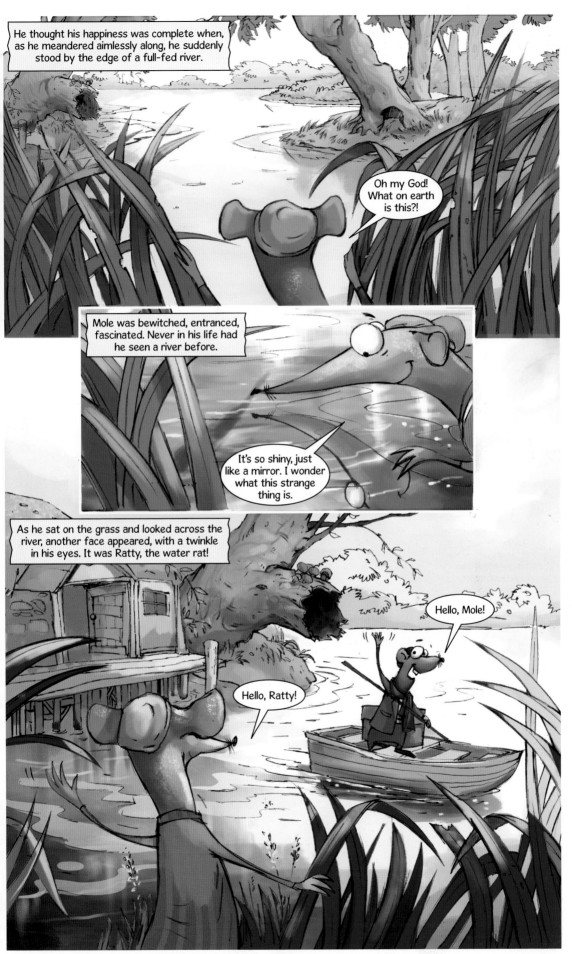

He thought his happiness was complete when, as he meandered aimlessly along, he suddenly stood by the edge of a full-fed river.

Oh my God! What on earth is this?!

Mole was bewitched, entranced, fascinated. Never in his life had he seen a river before.

It's so shiny, just like a mirror. I wonder what this strange thing is.

As he sat on the grass and looked across the river, another face appeared, with a twinkle in his eyes. It was Ratty, the water rat!

Hello, Mole!

Hello, Ratty!

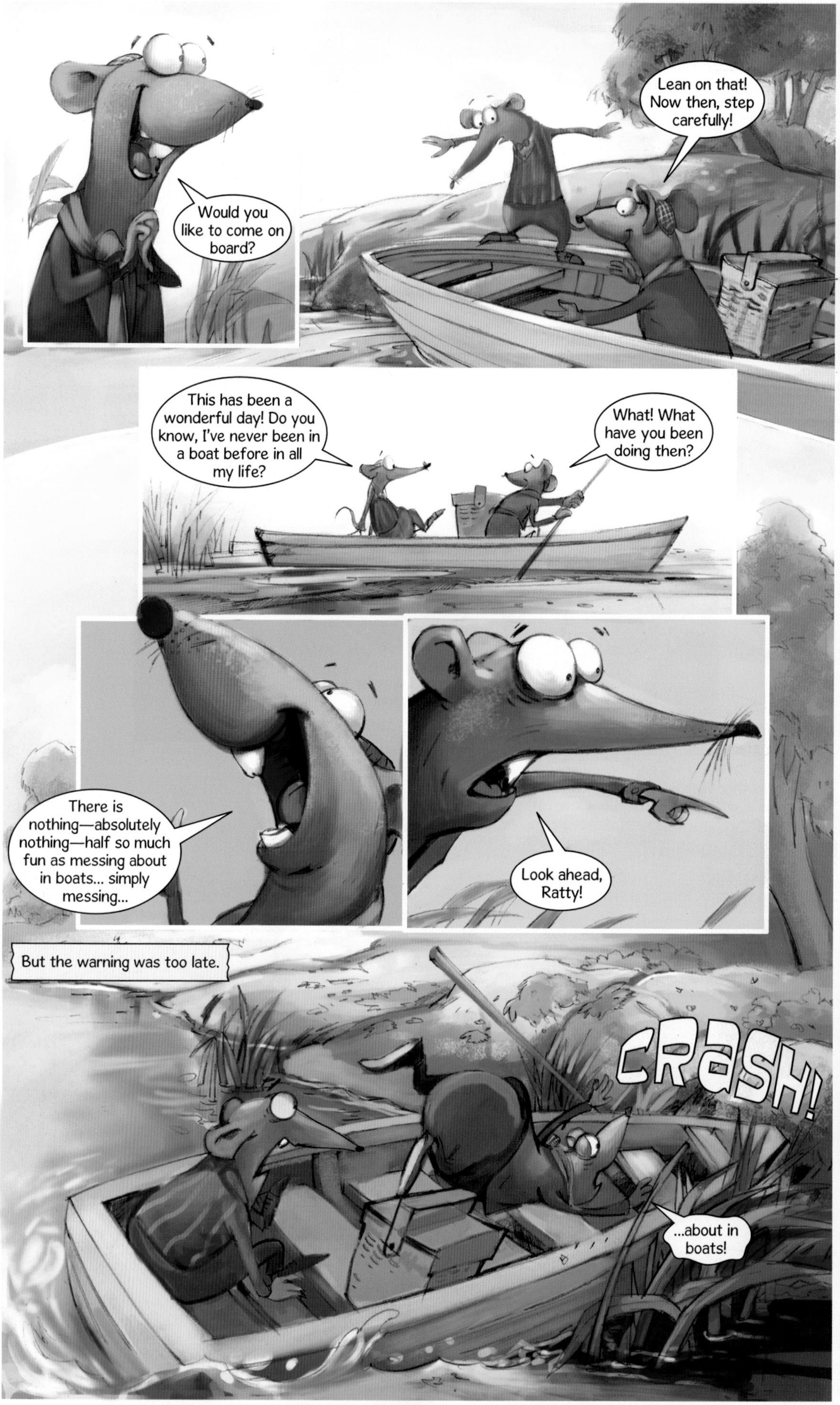

Would you like to come on board?
Lean on that! Now then, step carefully!
This has been a wonderful day! Do you know, I've never been in a boat before in all my life?
What! What have you been doing then?
There is nothing—absolutely nothing—half so much fun as messing about in boats... simply messing...
Look ahead, Ratty!
But the warning was too late.
CRASH!
...about in boats!

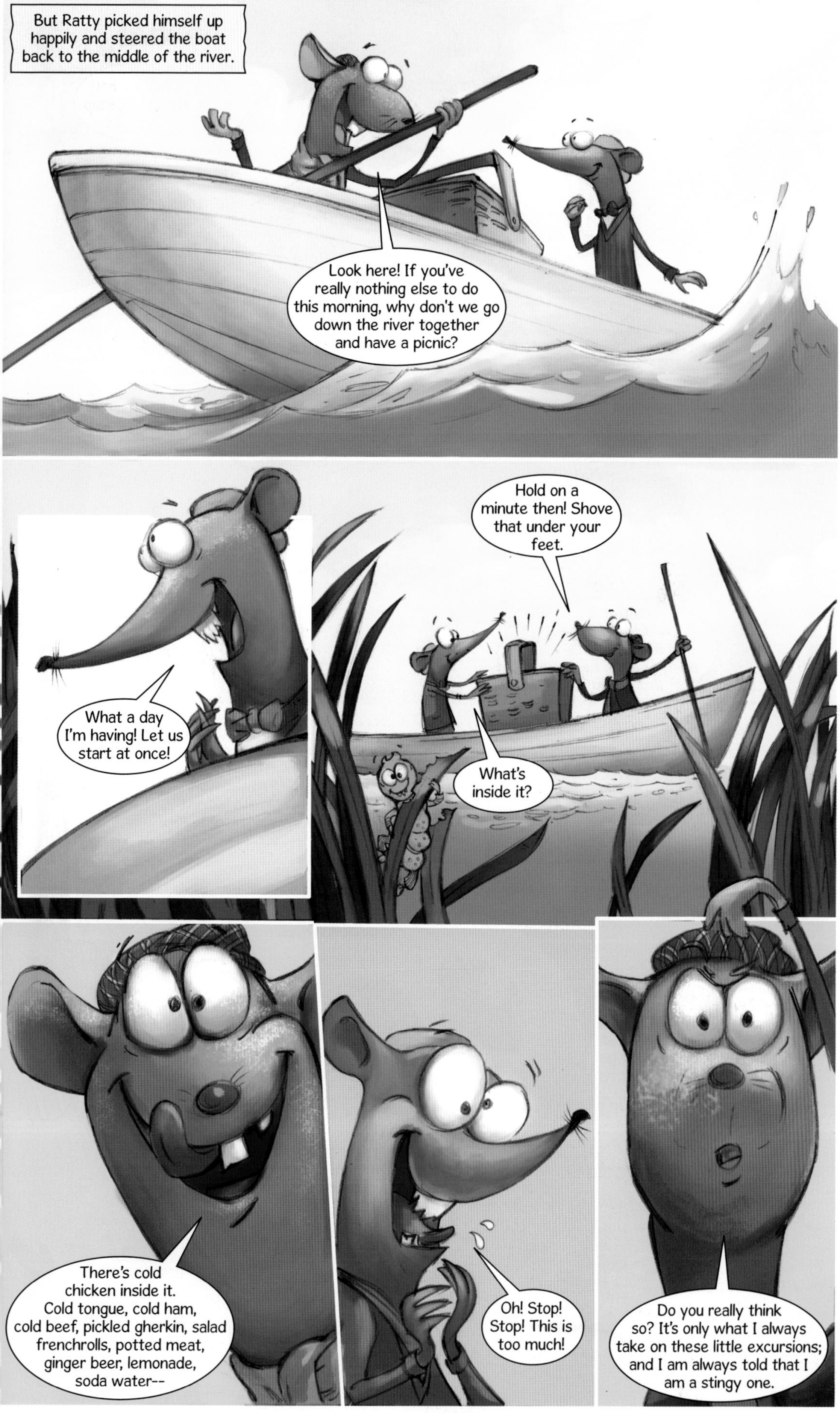
But Ratty picked himself up happily and steered the boat back to the middle of the river.
Look here! If you've really nothing else to do this morning, why don't we go down the river together and have a picnic?
What a day I'm having! Let us start at once!
Hold on a minute then! Shove that under your feet.
What's inside it?
There's cold chicken inside it. Cold tongue, cold ham, cold beef, pickled gherkin, salad frenchrolls, potted meat, ginger beer, lemonade, soda water--
Oh! Stop! Stop! This is too much!
Do you really think so? It's only what I always take on these little excursions; and I am always told that I am a stingy one.

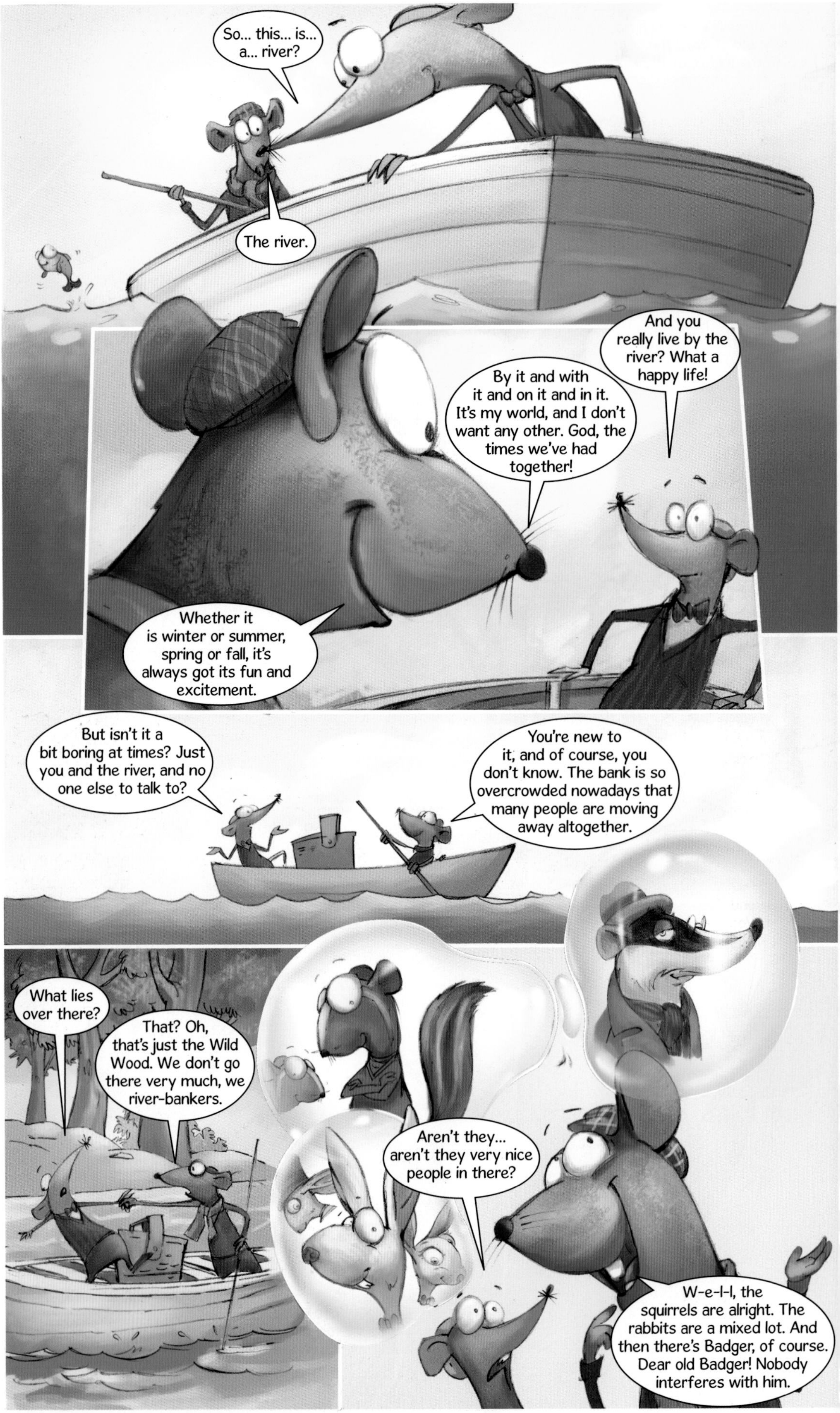
So... this... is... a... river?
The river.
And you really live by the river? What a happy life!
By it and with it and on it and in it. It's my world, and I don't want any other. God, the times we've had together!
Whether it is winter or summer, spring or fall, it's always got its fun and excitement.
But isn't it a bit boring at times? Just you and the river, and no one else to talk to?
You're new to it, and of course, you don't know. The bank is so overcrowded nowadays that many people are moving away altogether.
What lies over there?
That? Oh, that's just the Wild Wood. We don't go there very much, we river-bankers.
Aren't they... aren't they very nice people in there?
W-e-l-l, the squirrels are alright. The rabbits are a mixed lot. And then there's Badger, of course. Dear old Badger! Nobody interferes with him.

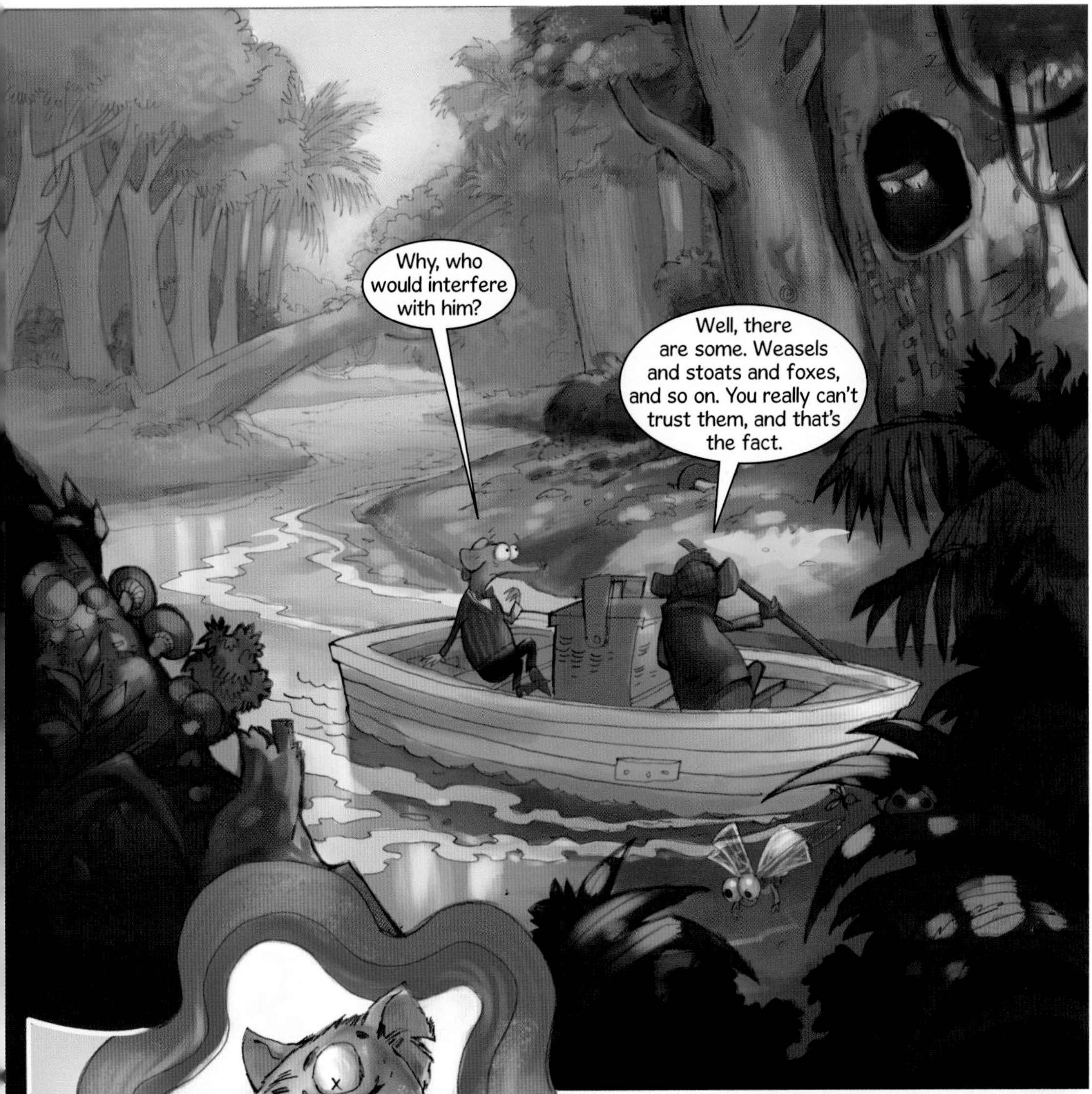
Why, who would interfere with him?
Well, there are some. Weasels and stoats and foxes, and so on. You really can't trust them, and that's the fact.

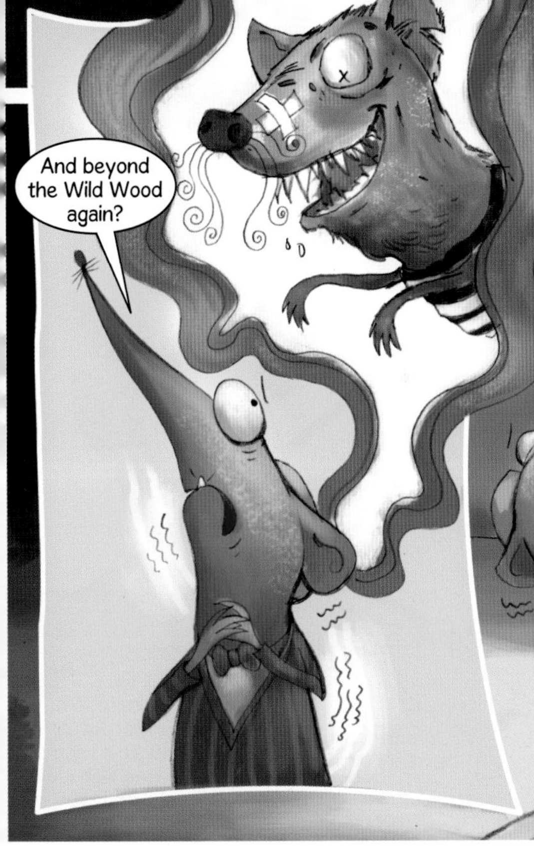
And beyond the Wild Wood again?

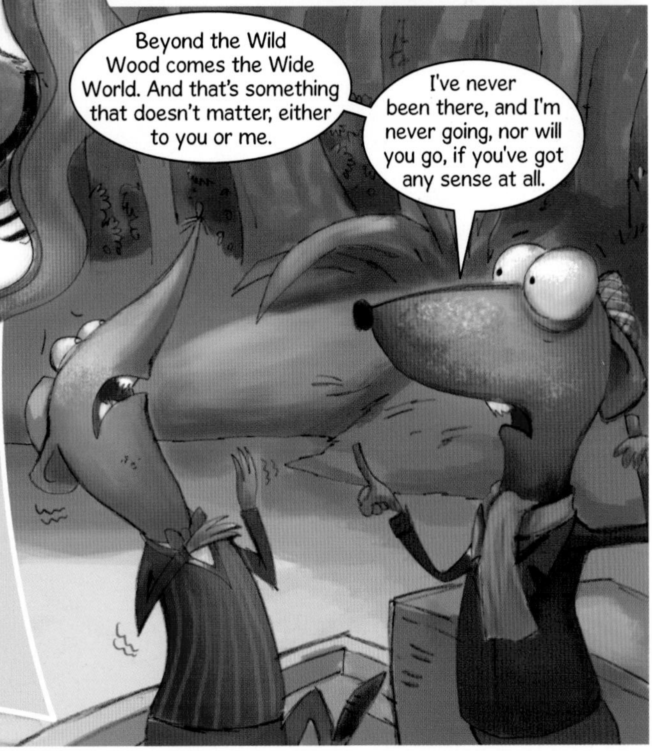
Beyond the Wild Wood comes the Wide World. And that's something that doesn't matter, either to you or me.
I've never been there, and I'm never going, nor will you go, if you've got any sense at all.

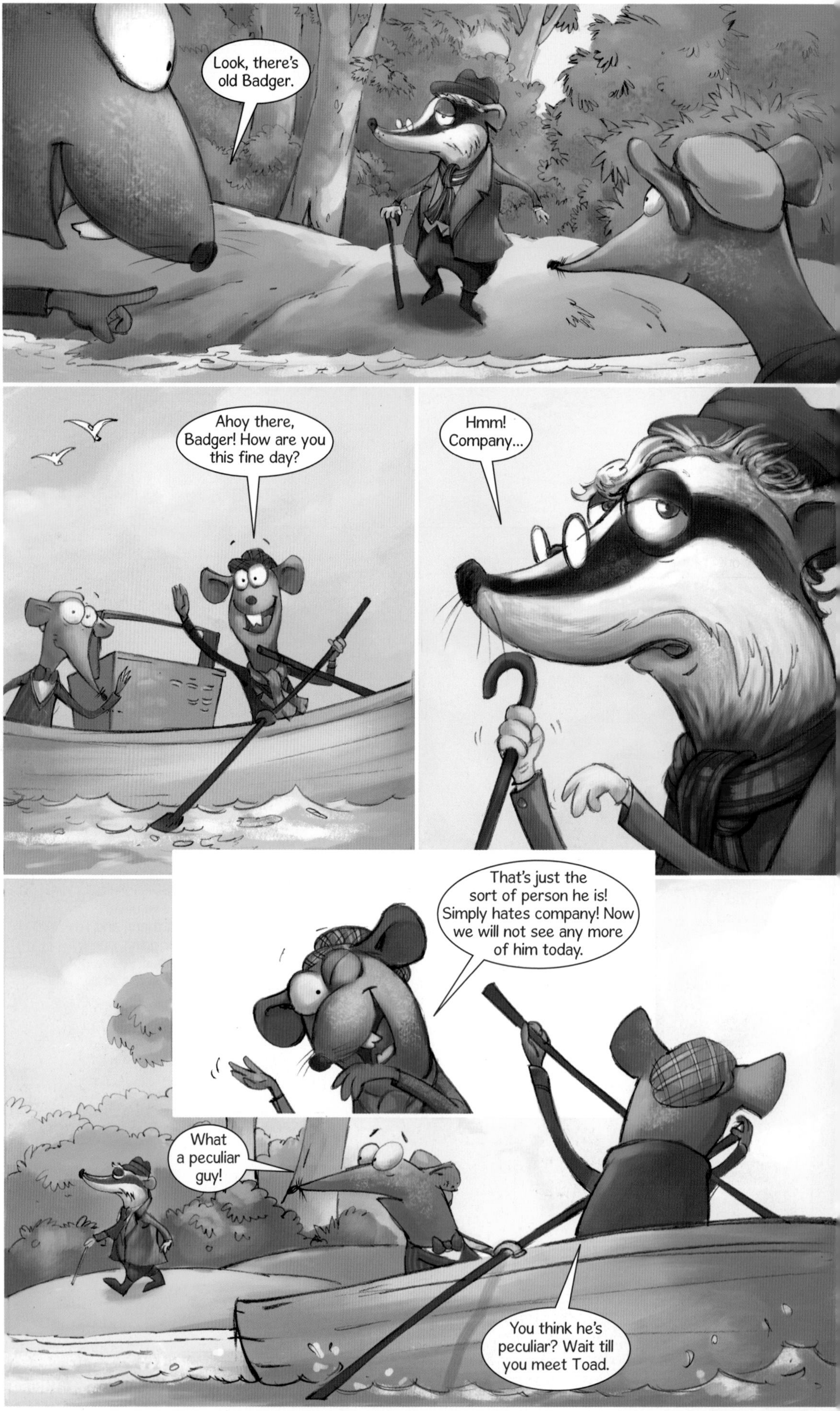
Look, there's old Badger.
Ahoy there, Badger! How are you this fine day?
Hmm! Company...
That's just the sort of person he is! Simply hates company! Now we will not see any more of him today.
What a peculiar guy!
You think he's peculiar? Wait till you meet Toad.

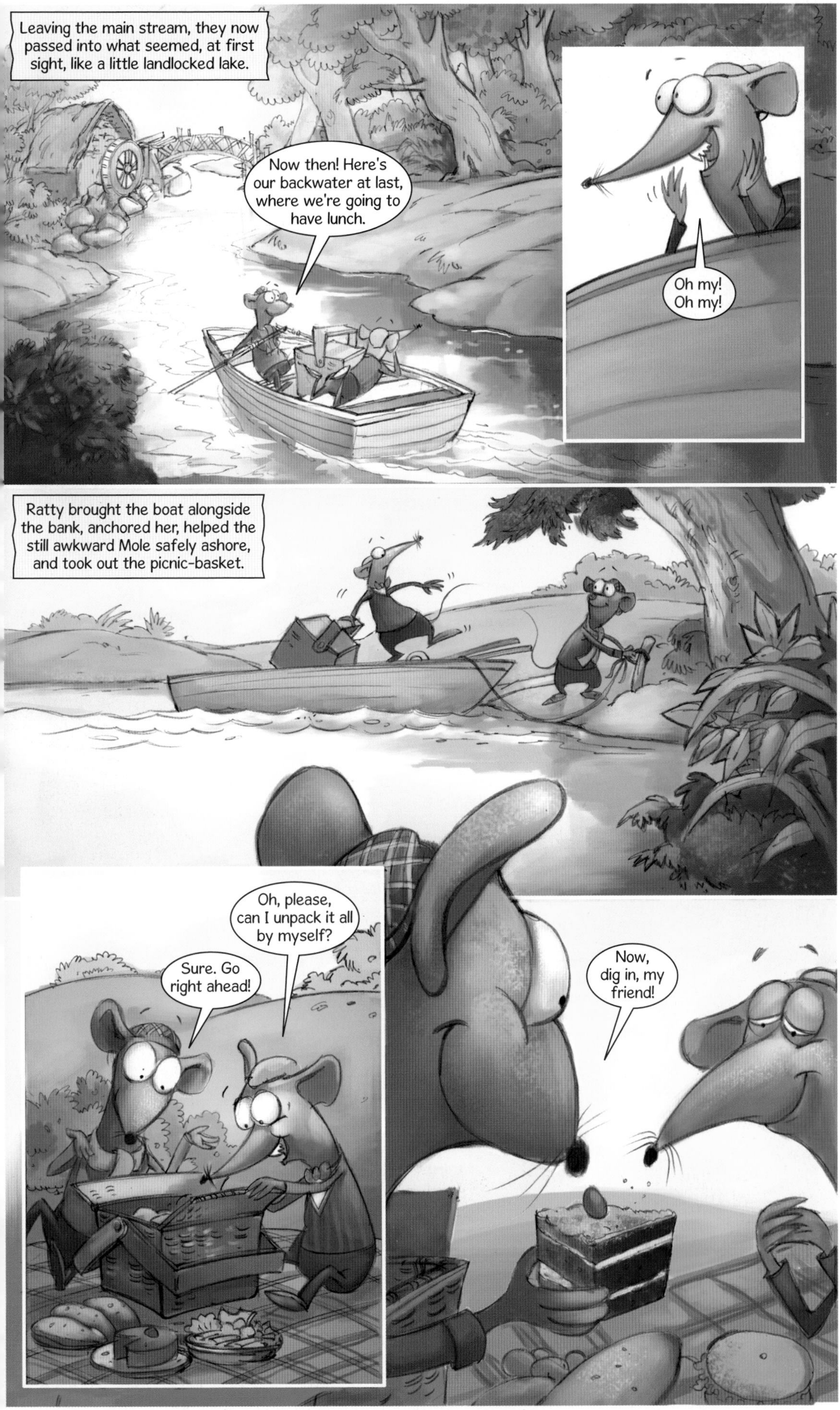

Leaving the main stream, they now passed into what seemed, at first sight, like a little landlocked lake.
Now then! Here's our backwater at last, where we're going to have lunch.
Oh my! Oh my!
Ratty brought the boat alongside the bank, anchored her, helped the still awkward Mole safely ashore, and took out the picnic-basket.
Oh, please, can I unpack it all by myself?
Sure. Go right ahead!
Now, dig in, my friend!

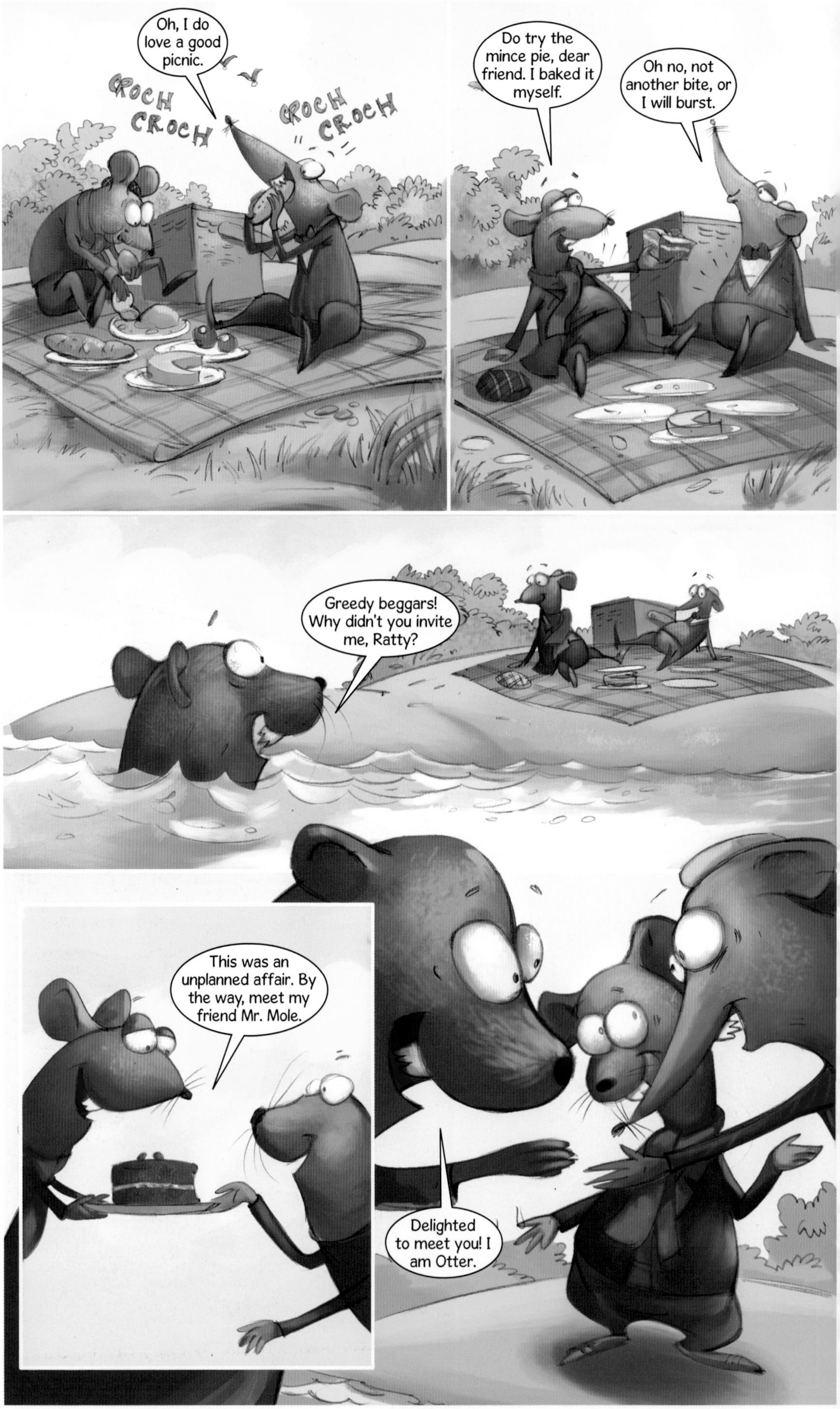
Oh, I do love a good picnic.
CROCH CROCH
CROCH CROCH
Do try the mince pie, dear friend. I baked it myself.
Oh no, not another bite, or I will burst.
Greedy beggars! Why didn't you invite me, Ratty?
This was an unplanned affair. By the way, meet my friend Mr. Mole.
Delighted to meet you! I am Otter.

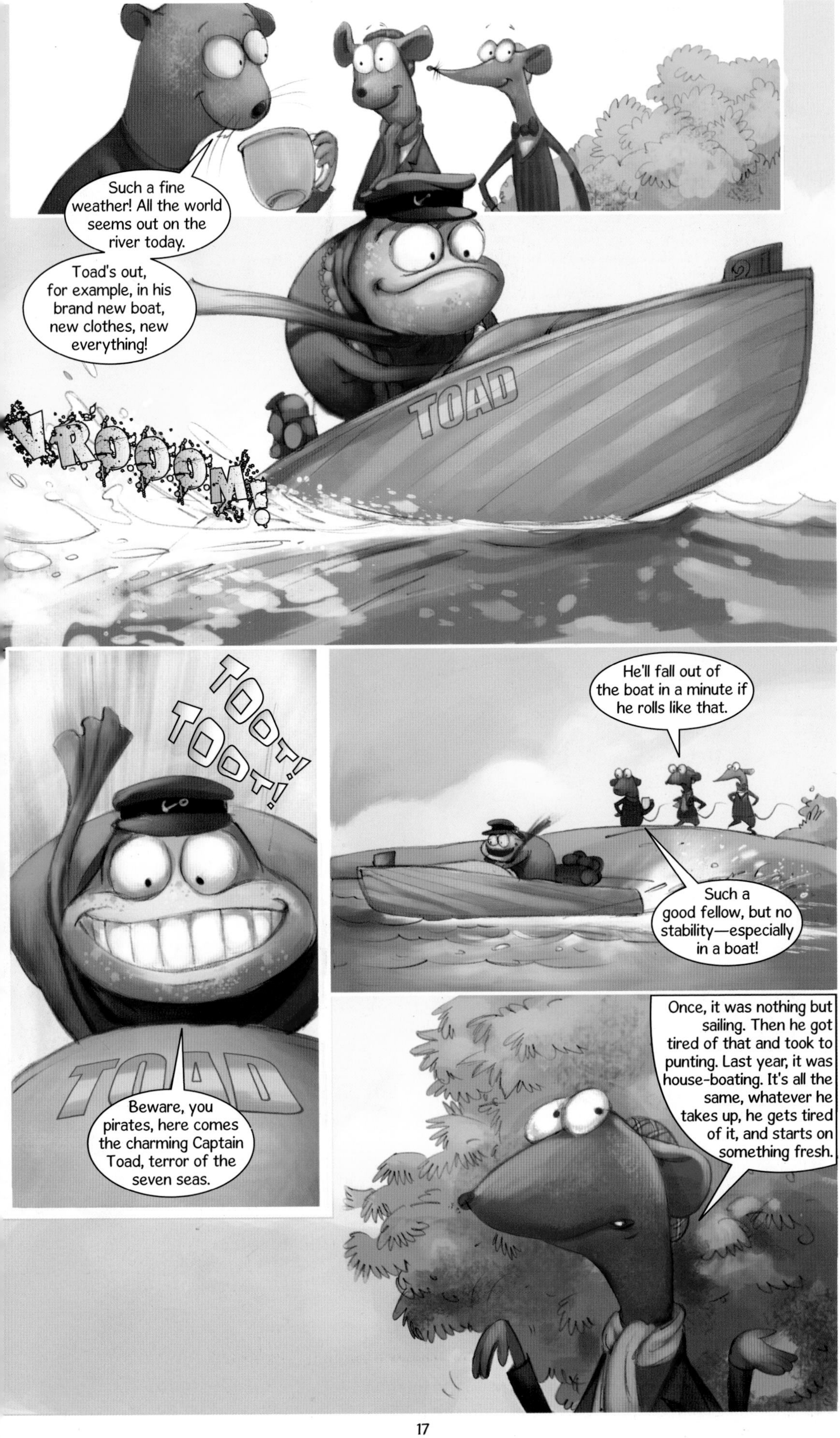

Such a fine weather! All the world seems out on the river today.
Toad's out, for example, in his brand new boat, new clothes, new everything!
VROOOOM!
TOAD
TOOT! TOOT!
Beware, you pirates, here comes the charming Captain Toad, terror of the seven seas.
TOAD
He'll fall out of the boat in a minute if he rolls like that.
Such a good fellow, but no stability—especially in a boat!
Once, it was nothing but sailing. Then he got tired of that and took to punting. Last year, it was house-boating. It's all the same, whatever he takes up, he gets tired of it, and starts on something fresh.

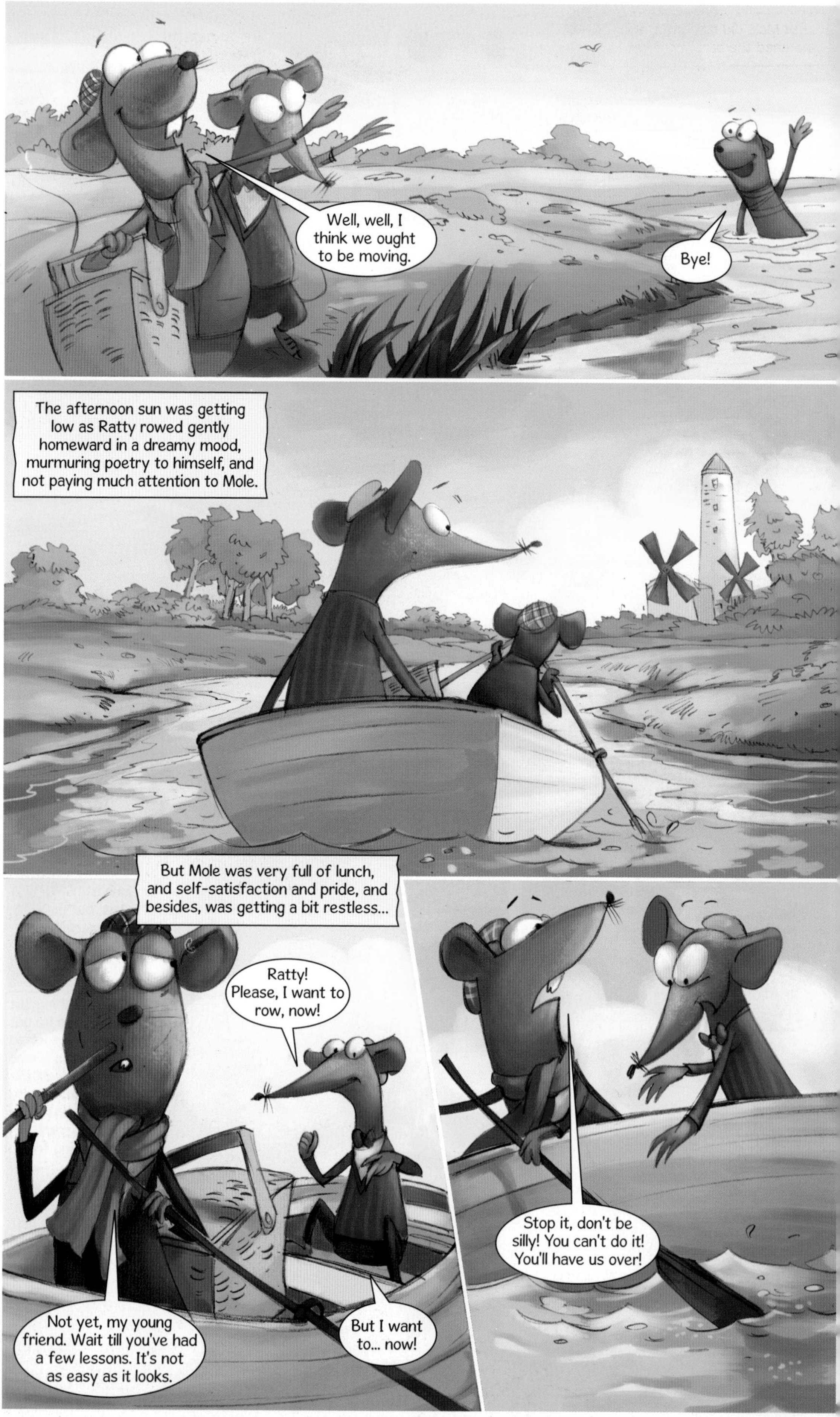

Well, well, I think we ought to be moving.
Bye!
The afternoon sun was getting low as Ratty rowed gently homeward in a dreamy mood, murmuring poetry to himself, and not paying much attention to Mole.
But Mole was very full of lunch, and self-satisfaction and pride, and besides, was getting a bit restless...
Ratty! Please, I want to row, now!
Not yet, my young friend. Wait till you've had a few lessons. It's not as easy as it looks.
But I want to... now!
Stop it, don't be silly! You can't do it! You'll have us over!

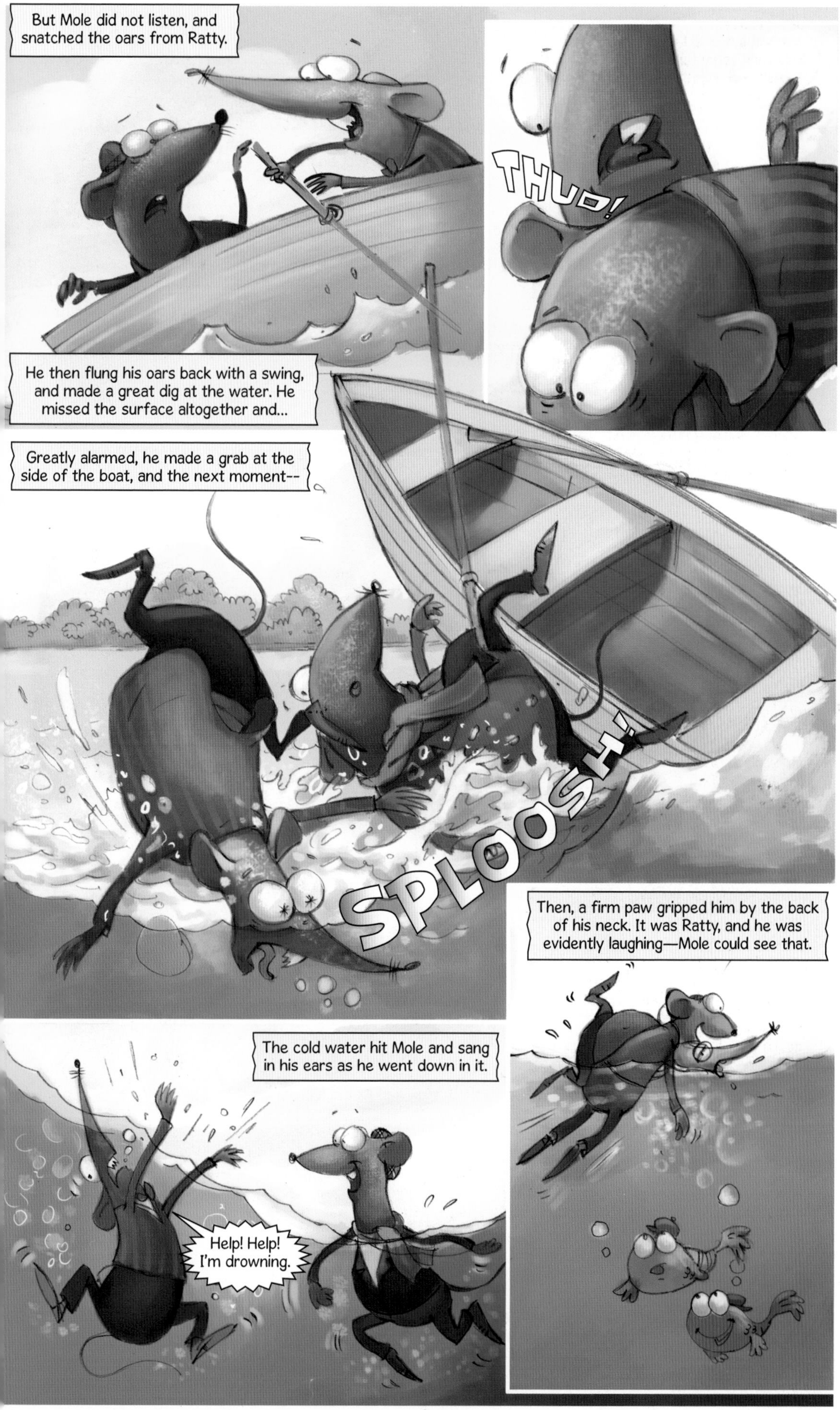
But Mole did not listen, and snatched the oars from Ratty.
THUD!
He then flung his oars back with a swing, and made a great dig at the water. He missed the surface altogether and...
Greatly alarmed, he made a grab at the side of the boat, and the next moment--
SPLOOSH!
The cold water hit Mole and sang in his ears as he went down in it.
Help! Help! I'm drowning.
Then, a firm paw gripped him by the back of his neck. It was Ratty, and he was evidently laughing—Mole could see that.

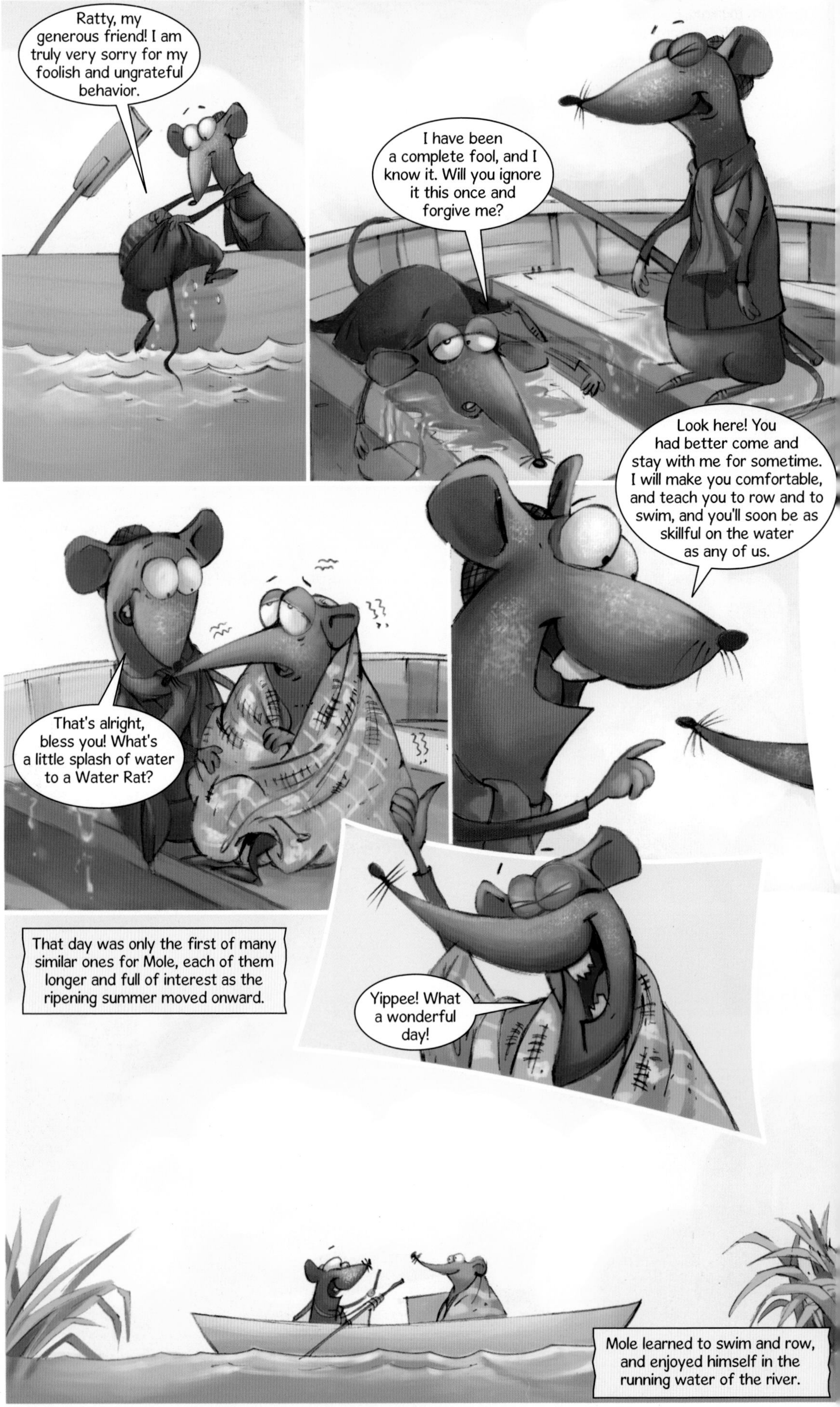

Ratty, my generous friend! I am truly very sorry for my foolish and ungrateful behavior.
I have been a complete fool, and I know it. Will you ignore it this once and forgive me?
That's alright, bless you! What's a little splash of water to a Water Rat?
Look here! You had better come and stay with me for sometime. I will make you comfortable, and teach you to row and to swim, and you'll soon be as skillful on the water as any of us.
That day was only the first of many similar ones for Mole, each of them longer and full of interest as the ripening summer moved onward.
Yippee! What a wonderful day!
Mole learned to swim and row, and enjoyed himself in the running water of the river.

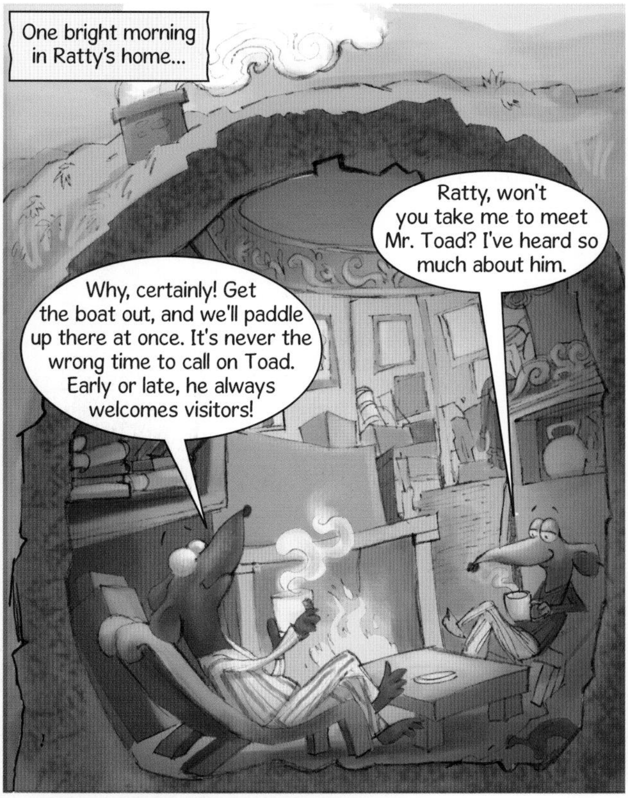
One bright morning in Ratty's home...
Ratty, won't you take me to meet Mr. Toad? I've heard so much about him.
Why, certainly! Get the boat out, and we'll paddle up there at once. It's never the wrong time to call on Toad. Early or late, he always welcomes visitors!

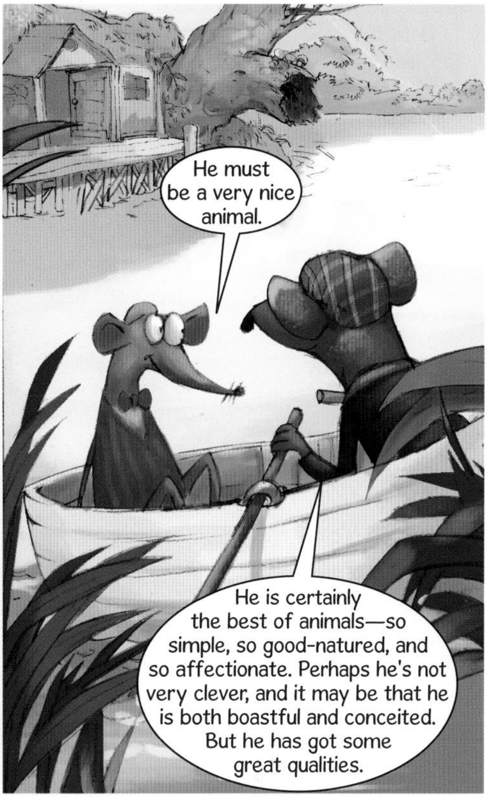
He must be a very nice animal.
He is certainly the best of animals—so simple, so good-natured, and so affectionate. Perhaps he's not very clever, and it may be that he is both boastful and conceited. But he has got some great qualities.

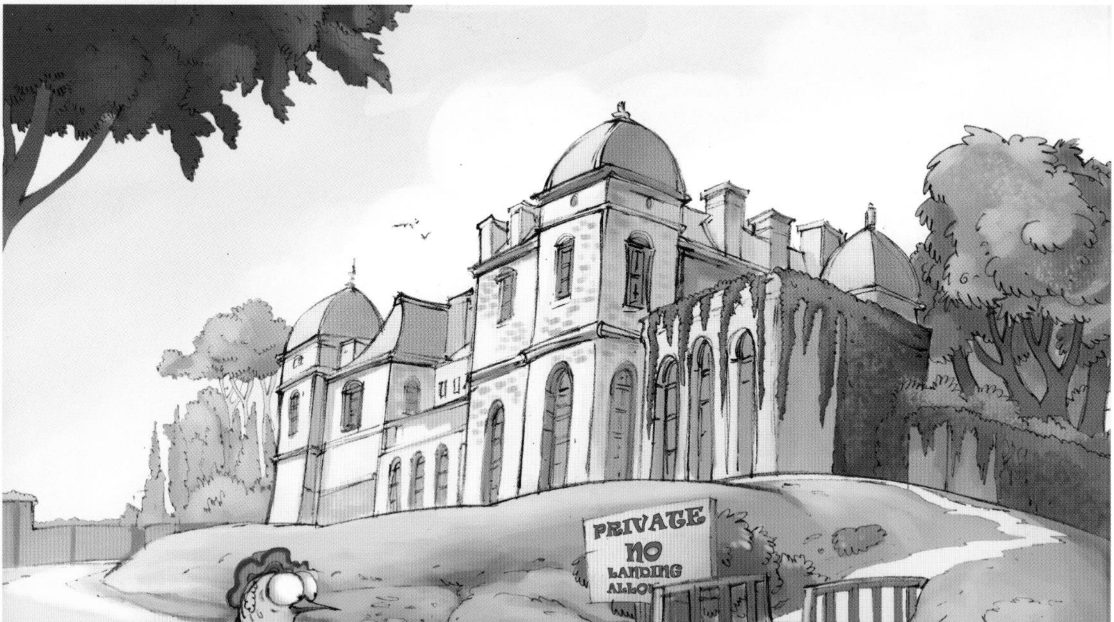
PRIVATE
NO
LANDING
ALLO
There's Toad Hall.

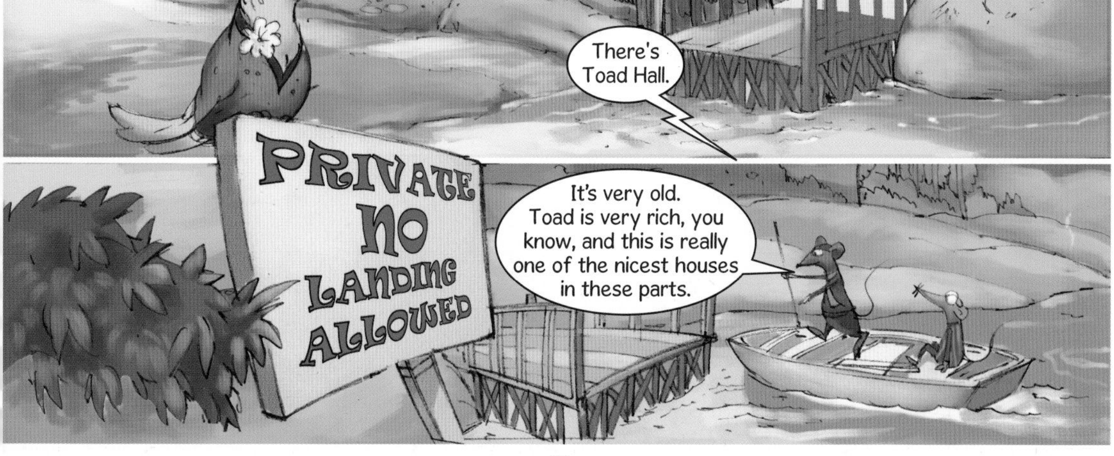
PRIVATE
NO
LANDING
ALLOWED
It's very old. Toad is very rich, you know, and this is really one of the nicest houses in these parts.

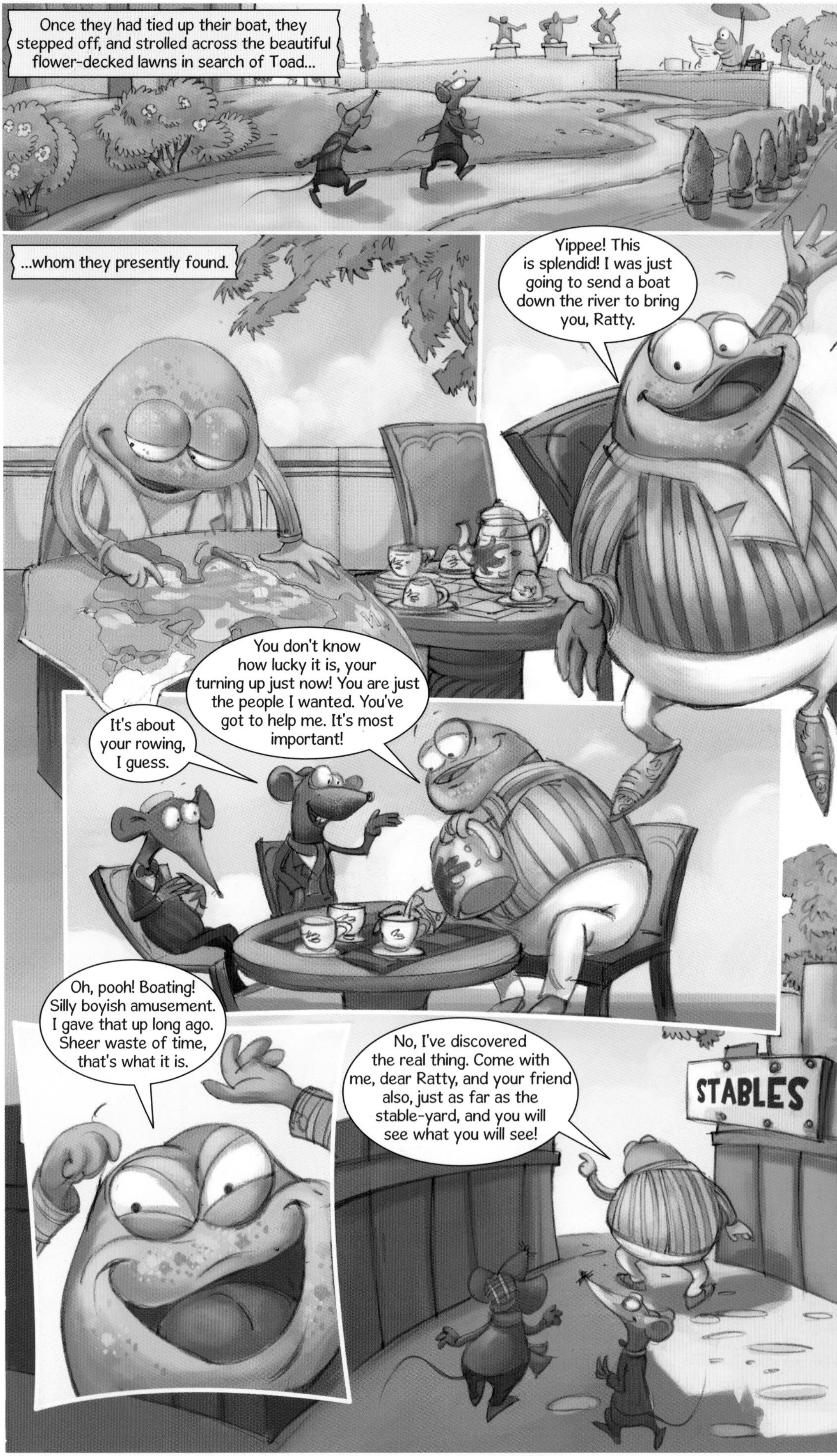
Once they had tied up their boat, they stepped off, and strolled across the beautiful flower-decked lawns in search of Toad...
...whom they presently found.
Yippee! This is splendid! I was just going to send a boat down the river to bring you, Ratty.
You don't know how lucky it is, your turning up just now! You are just the people I wanted. You've got to help me. It's most important!
It's about your rowing, I guess.
Oh, pooh! Boating! Silly boyish amusement. I gave that up long ago. Sheer waste of time, that's what it is.
No, I've discovered the real thing. Come with me, dear Ratty, and your friend also, just as far as the stable-yard, and you will see what you will see!
STABLES

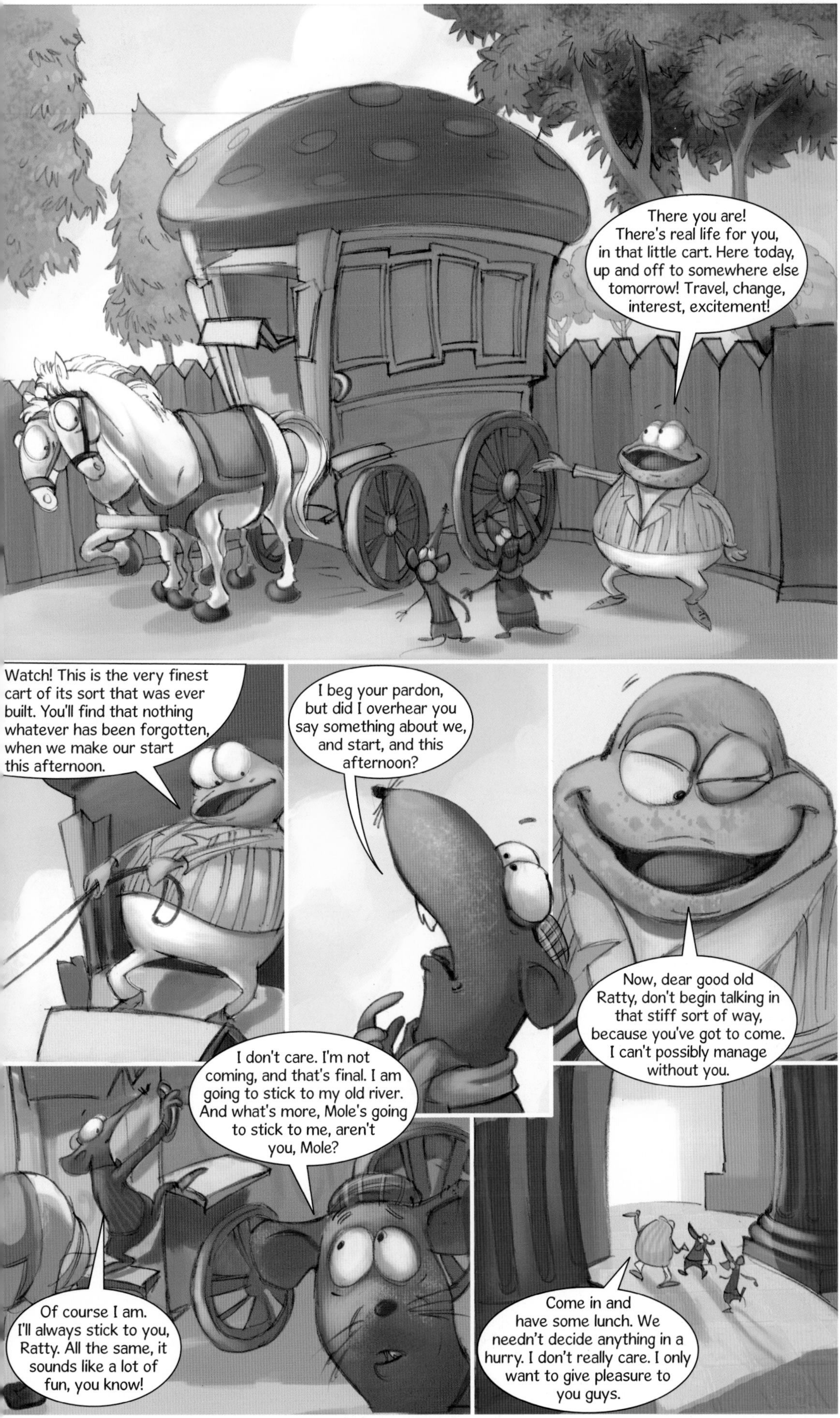
There you are! There's real life for you, in that little cart. Here today, up and off to somewhere else tomorrow! Travel, change, interest, excitement!
Watch! This is the very finest cart of its sort that was ever built. You'll find that nothing whatever has been forgotten, when we make our start this afternoon.
I beg your pardon, but did I overhear you say something about we, and start, and this afternoon?
Now, dear good old Ratty, don't begin talking in that stiff sort of way, because you've got to come. I can't possibly manage without you.
I don't care. I'm not coming, and that's final. I am going to stick to my old river. And what's more, Mole's going to stick to me, aren't you, Mole?
Of course I am. I'll always stick to you, Ratty. All the same, it sounds like a lot of fun, you know!
Come in and have some lunch. We needn't decide anything in a hurry. I don't really care. I only want to give pleasure to you guys.

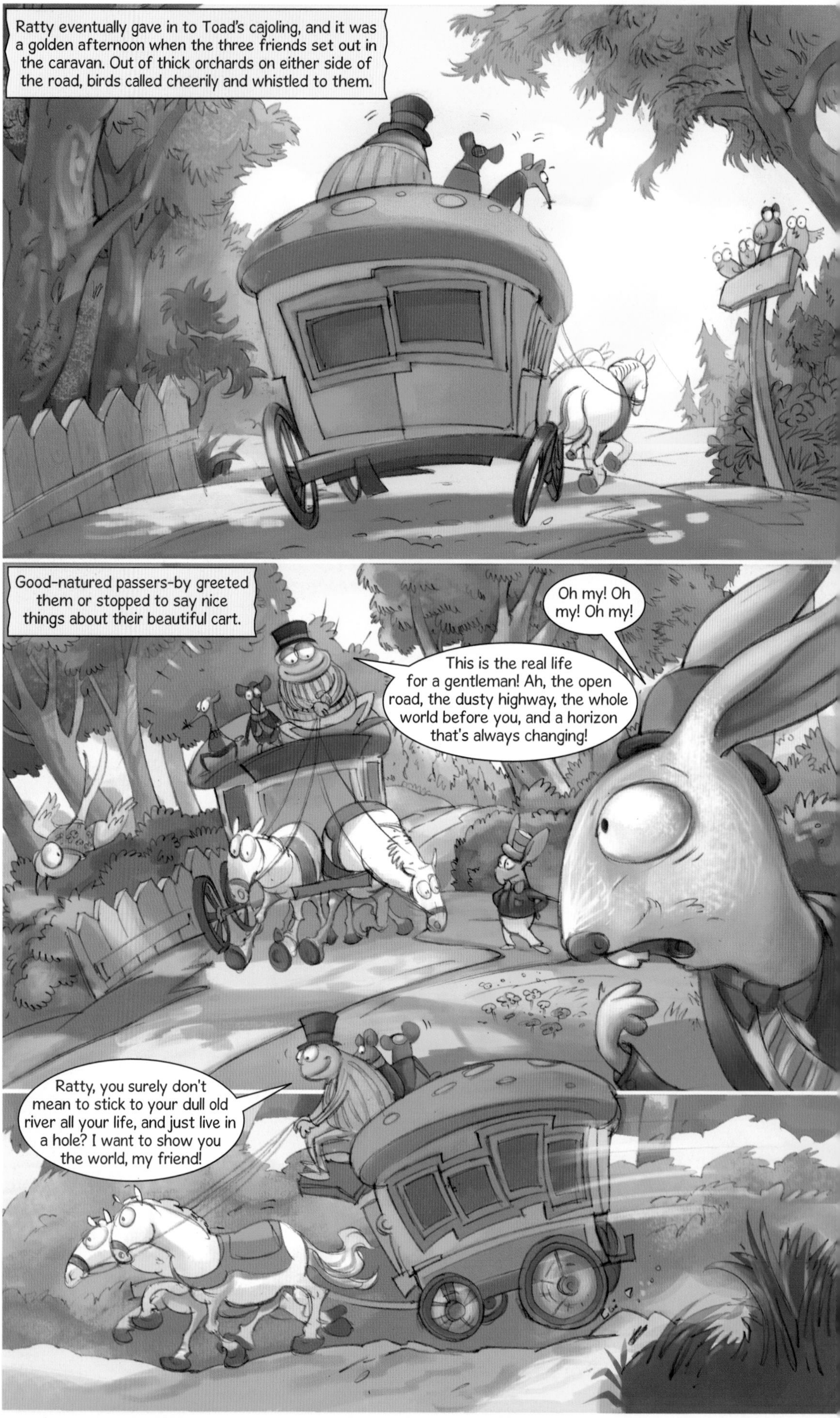
Ratty eventually gave in to Toad's cajoling, and it was a golden afternoon when the three friends set out in the caravan. Out of thick orchards on either side of the road, birds called cheerily and whistled to them.
Good-natured passers-by greeted them or stopped to say nice things about their beautiful cart.
Oh my! Oh my! Oh my!
This is the real life for a gentleman! Ah, the open road, the dusty highway, the whole world before you, and a horizon that's always changing!
Ratty, you surely don't mean to stick to your dull old river all your life, and just live in a hole? I want to show you the world, my friend!

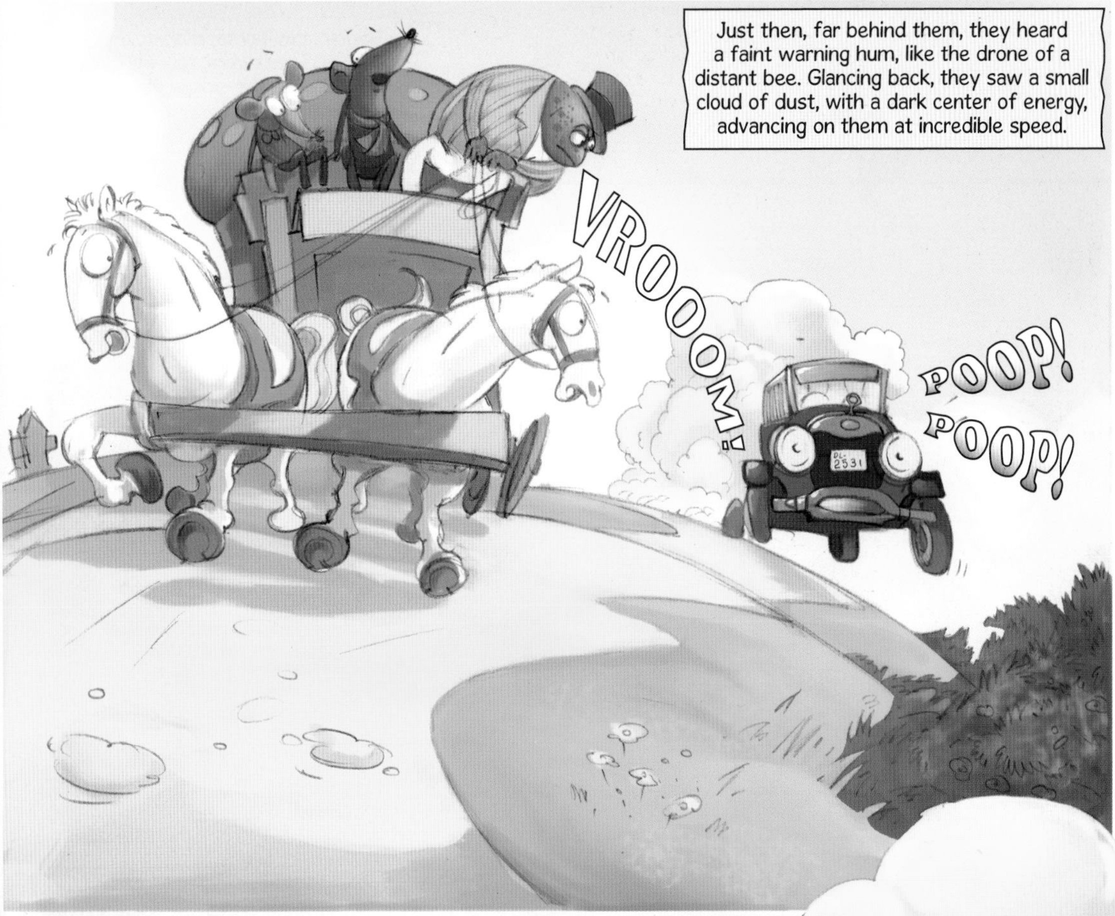
Just then, far behind them, they heard a faint warning hum, like the drone of a distant bee. Glancing back, they saw a small cloud of dust, with a dark center of energy, advancing on them at incredible speed.
VROOOOM!
POOP! POOP!

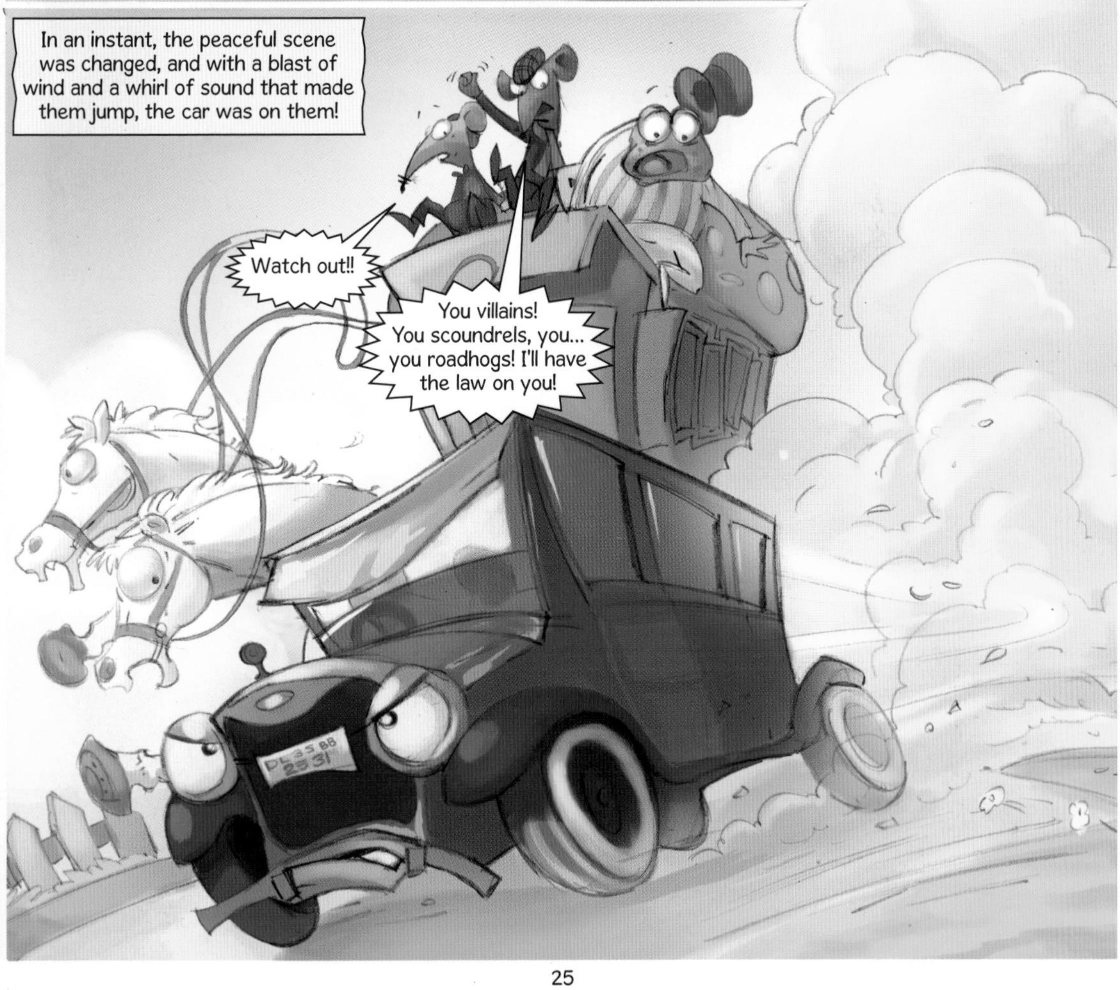
In an instant, the peaceful scene was changed, and with a blast of wind and a whirl of sound that made them jump, the car was on them!
Watch out!!
You villains! You scoundrels, you... you roadhogs! I'll have the law on you!

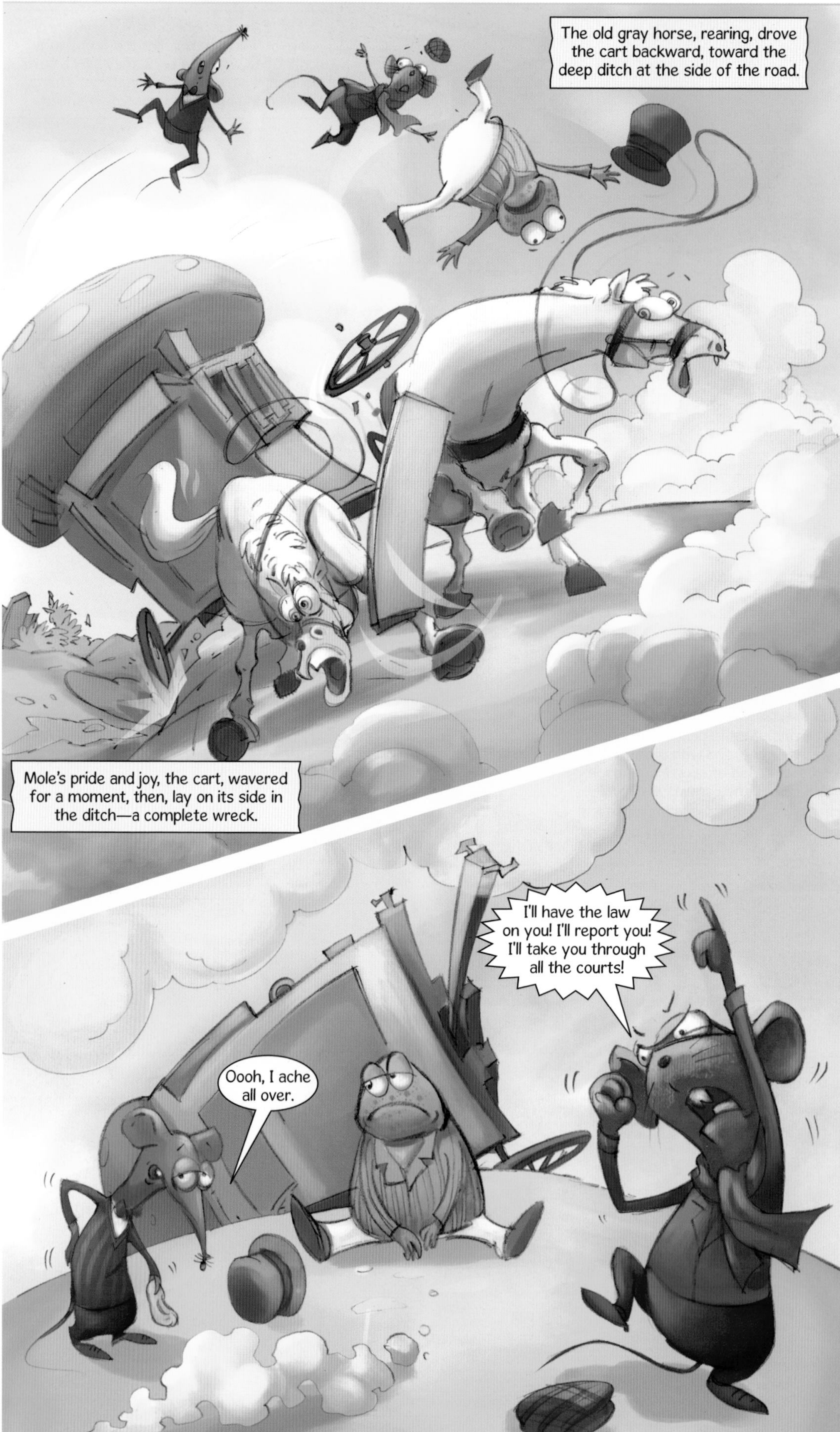
The old gray horse, rearing, drove the cart backward, toward the deep ditch at the side of the road.
Mole's pride and joy, the cart, wavered for a moment, then, lay on its side in the ditch—a complete wreck.
I'll have the law on you! I'll report you! I'll take you through all the courts!
Oooh, I ache all over.

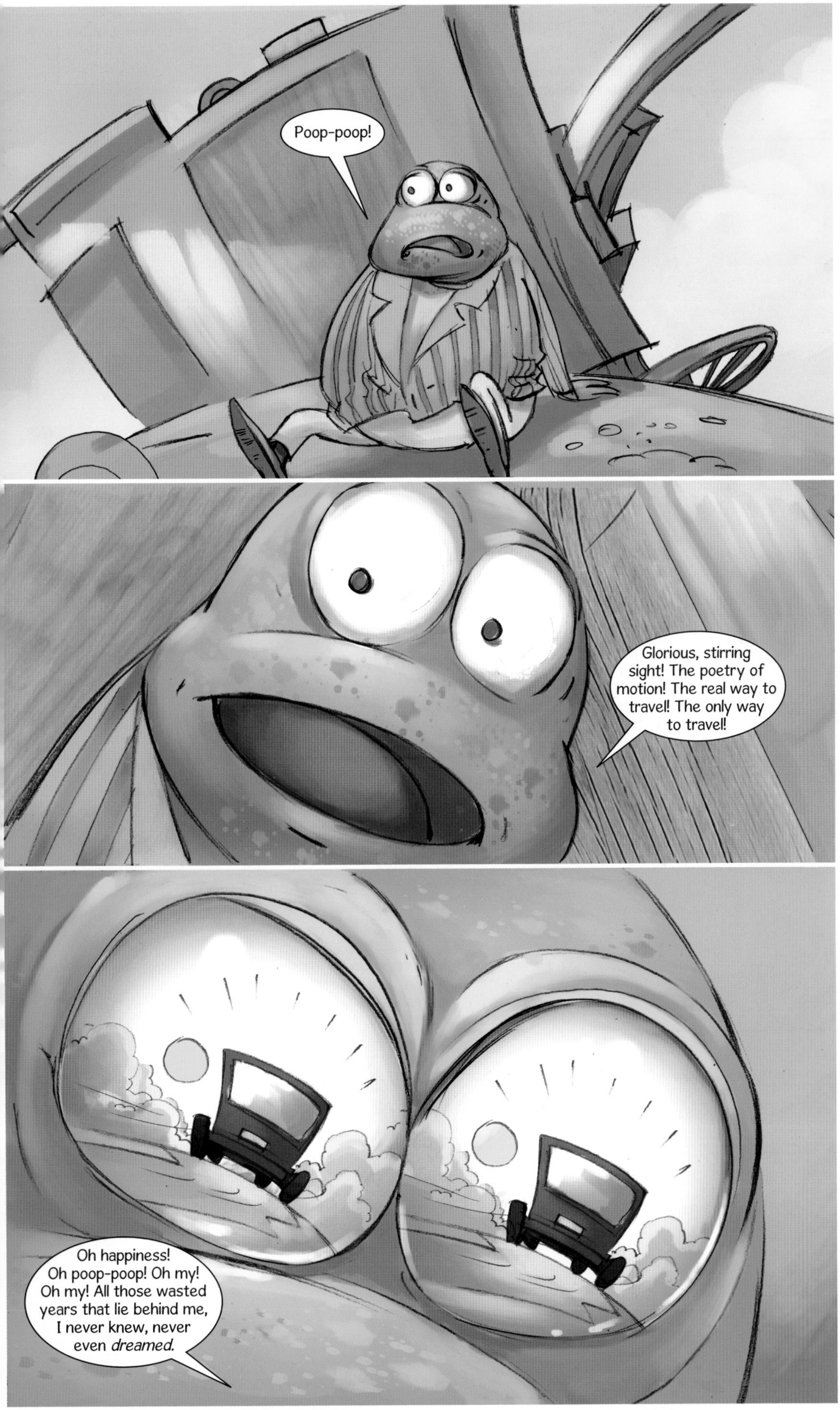
Poop-poop!
Glorious, stirring sight! The poetry of motion! The real way to travel! The only way to travel!
Oh happiness! Oh poop-poop! Oh my! Oh my! All those wasted years that lie behind me, I never knew, never even *dreamed.*

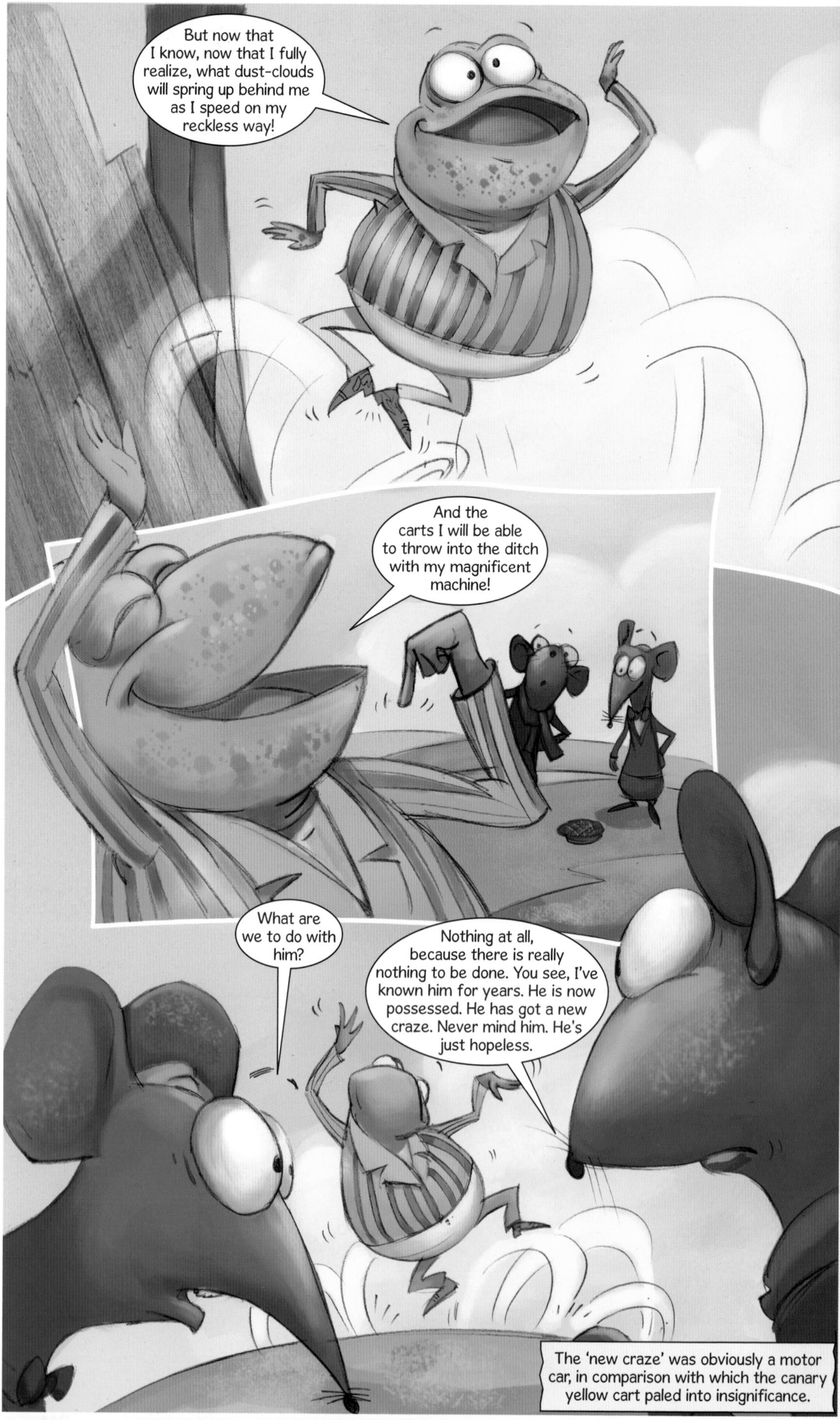
But now that I know, now that I fully realize, what dust-clouds will spring up behind me as I speed on my reckless way!
And the carts I will be able to throw into the ditch with my magnificent machine!
What are we to do with him?
Nothing at all, because there is really nothing to be done. You see, I've known him for years. He is now possessed. He has got a new craze. Never mind him. He's just hopeless.
The 'new craze' was obviously a motor car, in comparison with which the canary yellow cart paled into insignificance.

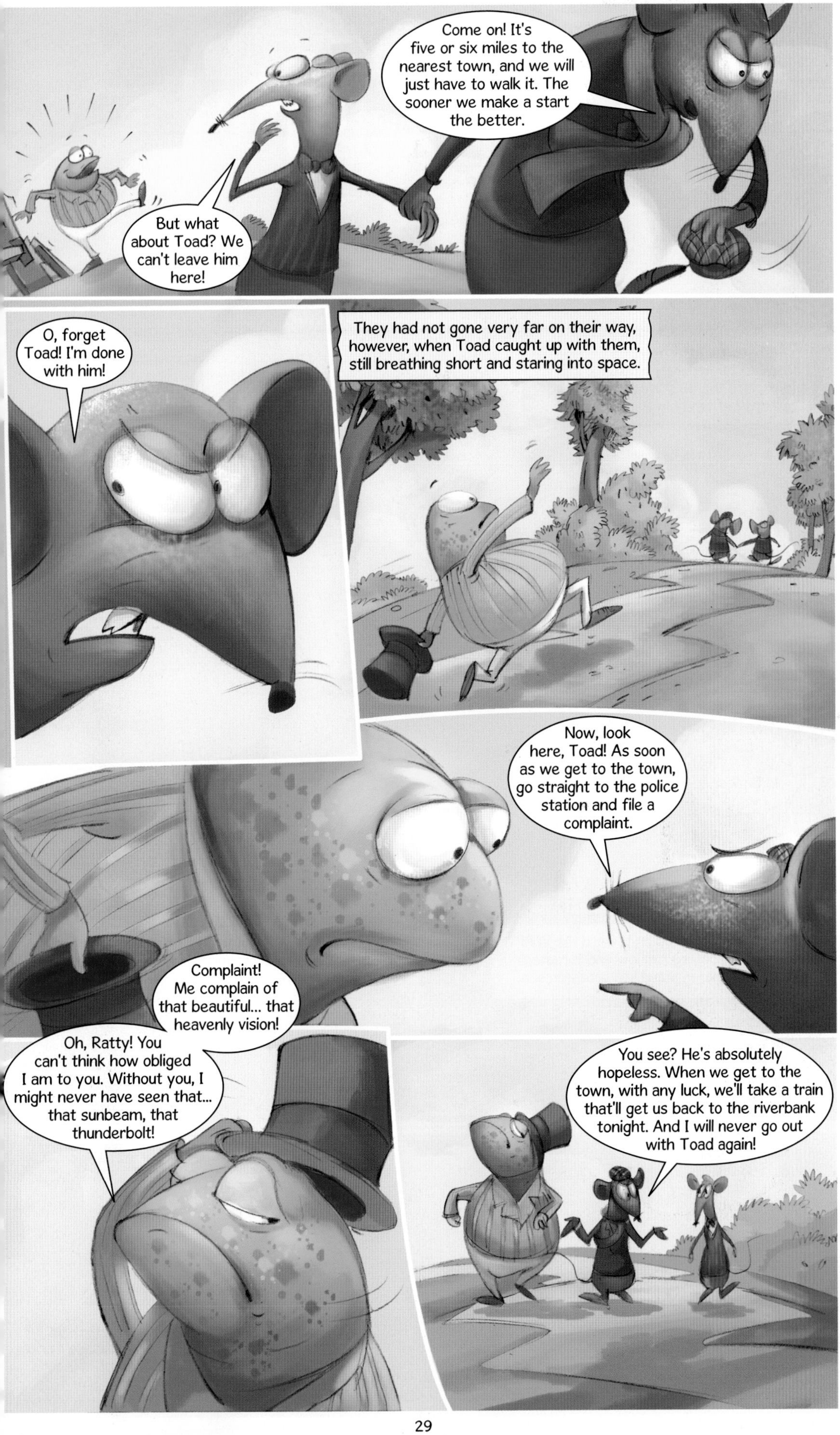
Come on! It's five or six miles to the nearest town, and we will just have to walk it. The sooner we make a start the better.
But what about Toad? We can't leave him here!
O, forget Toad! I'm done with him!
They had not gone very far on their way, however, when Toad caught up with them, still breathing short and staring into space.
Now, look here, Toad! As soon as we get to the town, go straight to the police station and file a complaint.
Complaint! Me complain of that beautiful... that heavenly vision!
Oh, Ratty! You can't think how obliged I am to you. Without you, I might never have seen that... that sunbeam, that thunderbolt!
You see? He's absolutely hopeless. When we get to the town, with any luck, we'll take a train that'll get us back to the riverbank tonight. And I will never go out with Toad again!

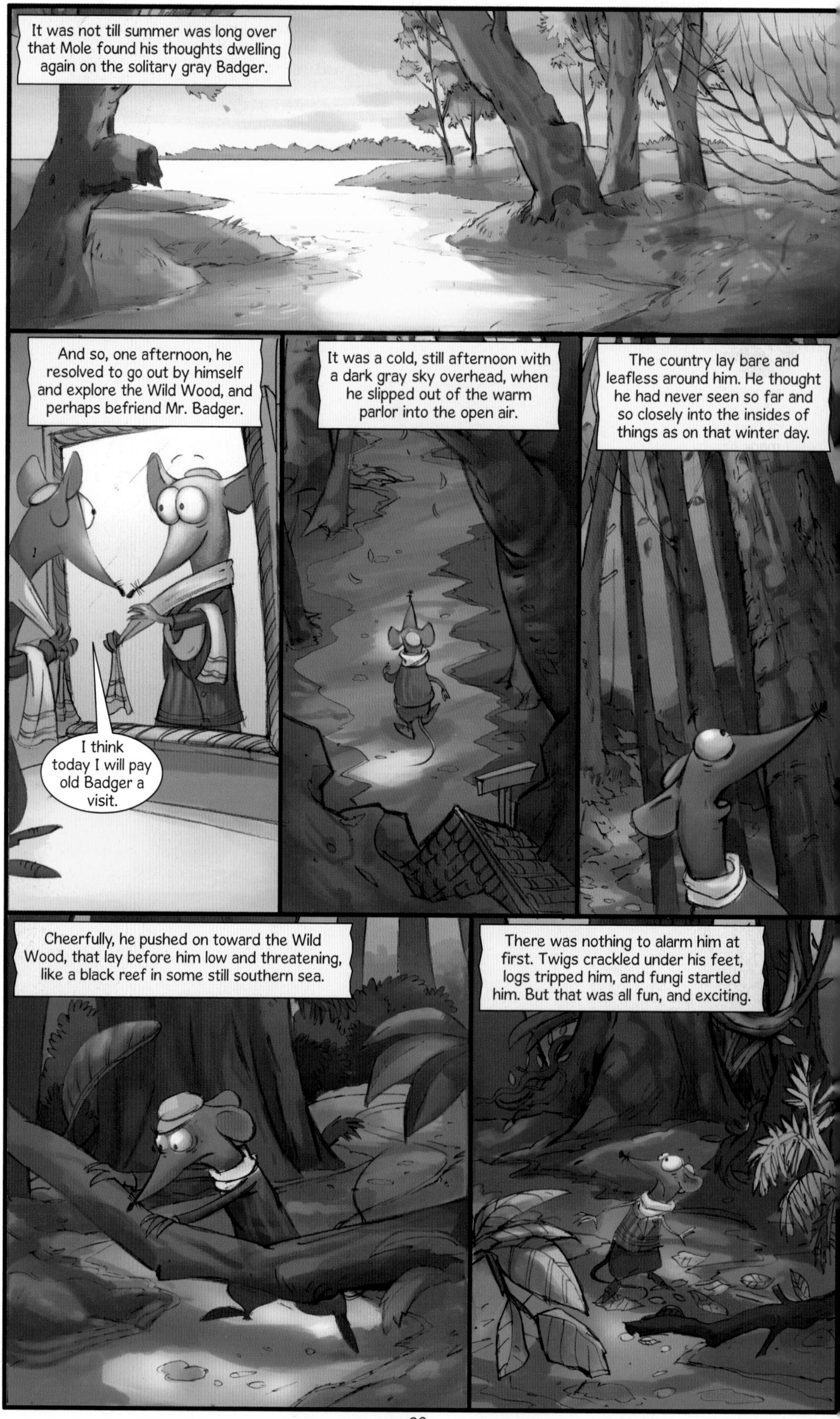
It was not till summer was long over that Mole found his thoughts dwelling again on the solitary gray Badger.
And so, one afternoon, he resolved to go out by himself and explore the Wild Wood, and perhaps befriend Mr. Badger.
I think today I will pay old Badger a visit.
It was a cold, still afternoon with a dark gray sky overhead, when he slipped out of the warm parlor into the open air.
The country lay bare and leafless around him. He thought he had never seen so far and so closely into the insides of things as on that winter day.
Cheerfully, he pushed on toward the Wild Wood, that lay before him low and threatening, like a black reef in some still southern sea.
There was nothing to alarm him at first. Twigs crackled under his feet, logs tripped him, and fungi startled him. But that was all fun, and exciting.

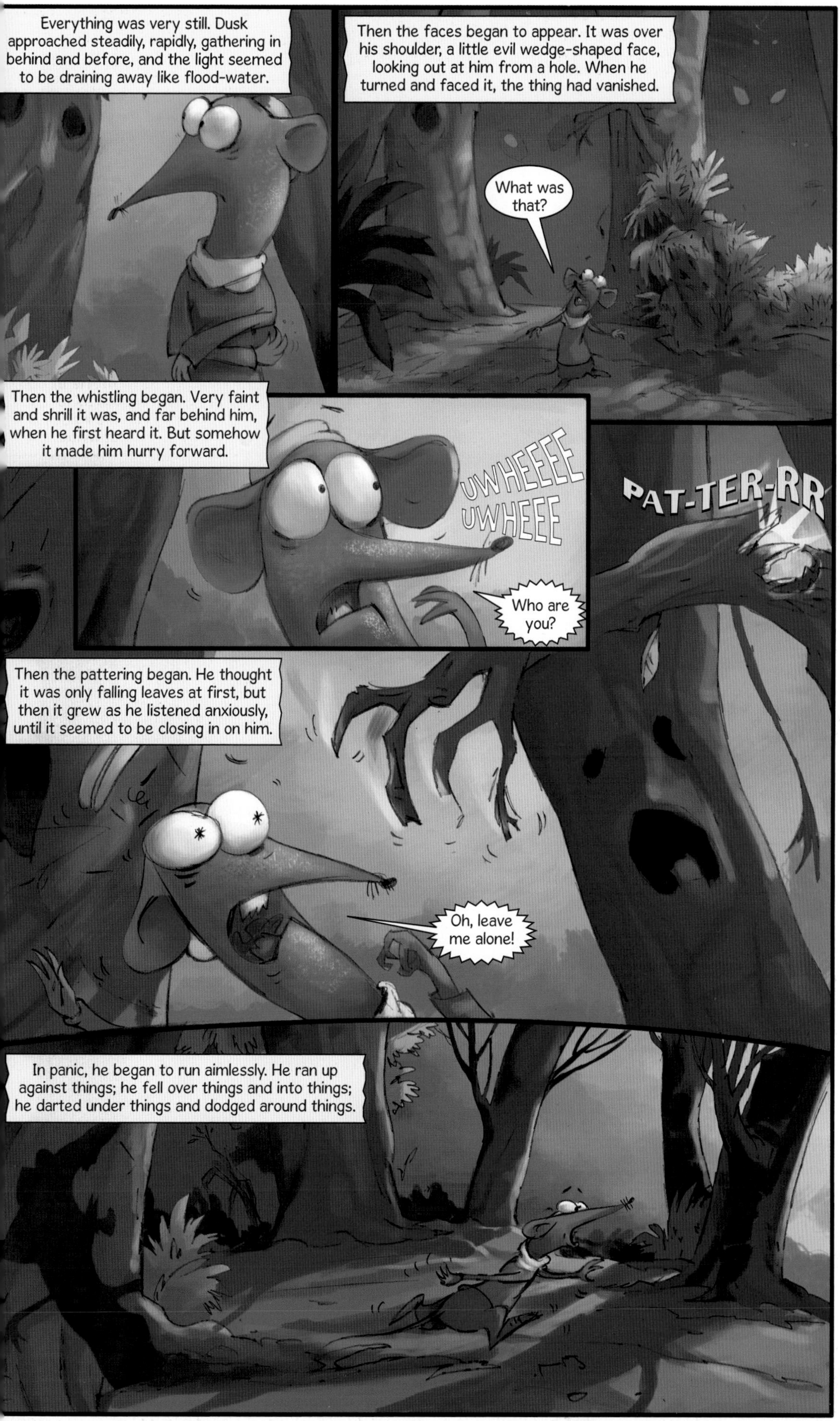
Everything was very still. Dusk approached steadily, rapidly, gathering in behind and before, and the light seemed to be draining away like flood-water.
Then the faces began to appear. It was over his shoulder, a little evil wedge-shaped face, looking out at him from a hole. When he turned and faced it, the thing had vanished.
What was that?
Then the whistling began. Very faint and shrill it was, and far behind him, when he first heard it. But somehow it made him hurry forward.
UWHEEEE
UWHEEE
Who are you?
PAT-TER-RR
Then the pattering began. He thought it was only falling leaves at first, but then it grew as he listened anxiously, until it seemed to be closing in on him.
Oh, leave me alone!
In panic, he began to run aimlessly. He ran up against things; he fell over things and into things; he darted under things and dodged around things.

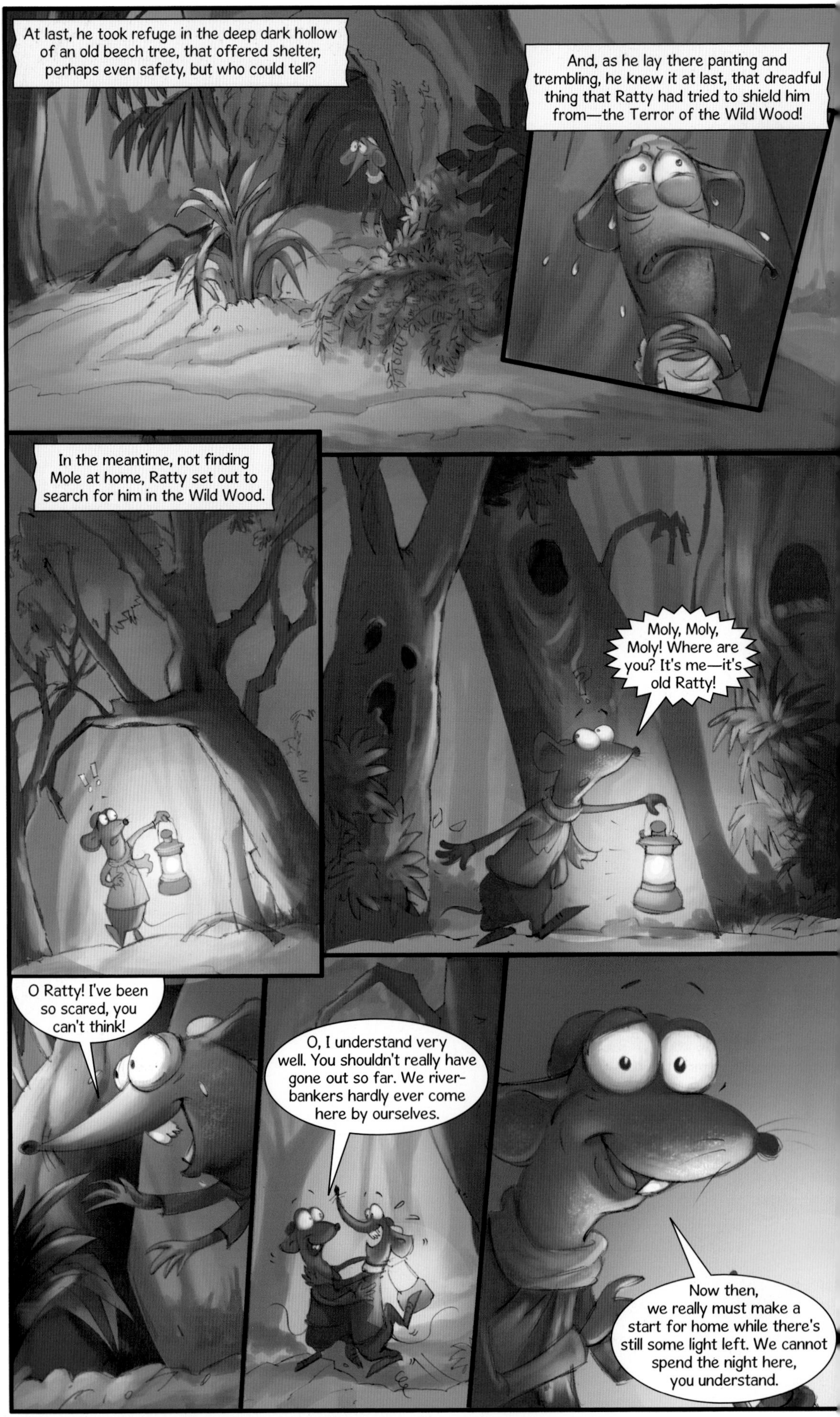

At last, he took refuge in the deep dark hollow of an old beech tree, that offered shelter, perhaps even safety, but who could tell?
And, as he lay there panting and trembling, he knew it at last, that dreadful thing that Ratty had tried to shield him from—the Terror of the Wild Wood!
In the meantime, not finding Mole at home, Ratty set out to search for him in the Wild Wood.
Moly, Moly, Moly! Where are you? It's me—it's old Ratty!
O Ratty! I've been so scared, you can't think!
O, I understand very well. You shouldn't really have gone out so far. We river-bankers hardly ever come here by ourselves.
Now then, we really must make a start for home while there's still some light left. We cannot spend the night here, you understand.

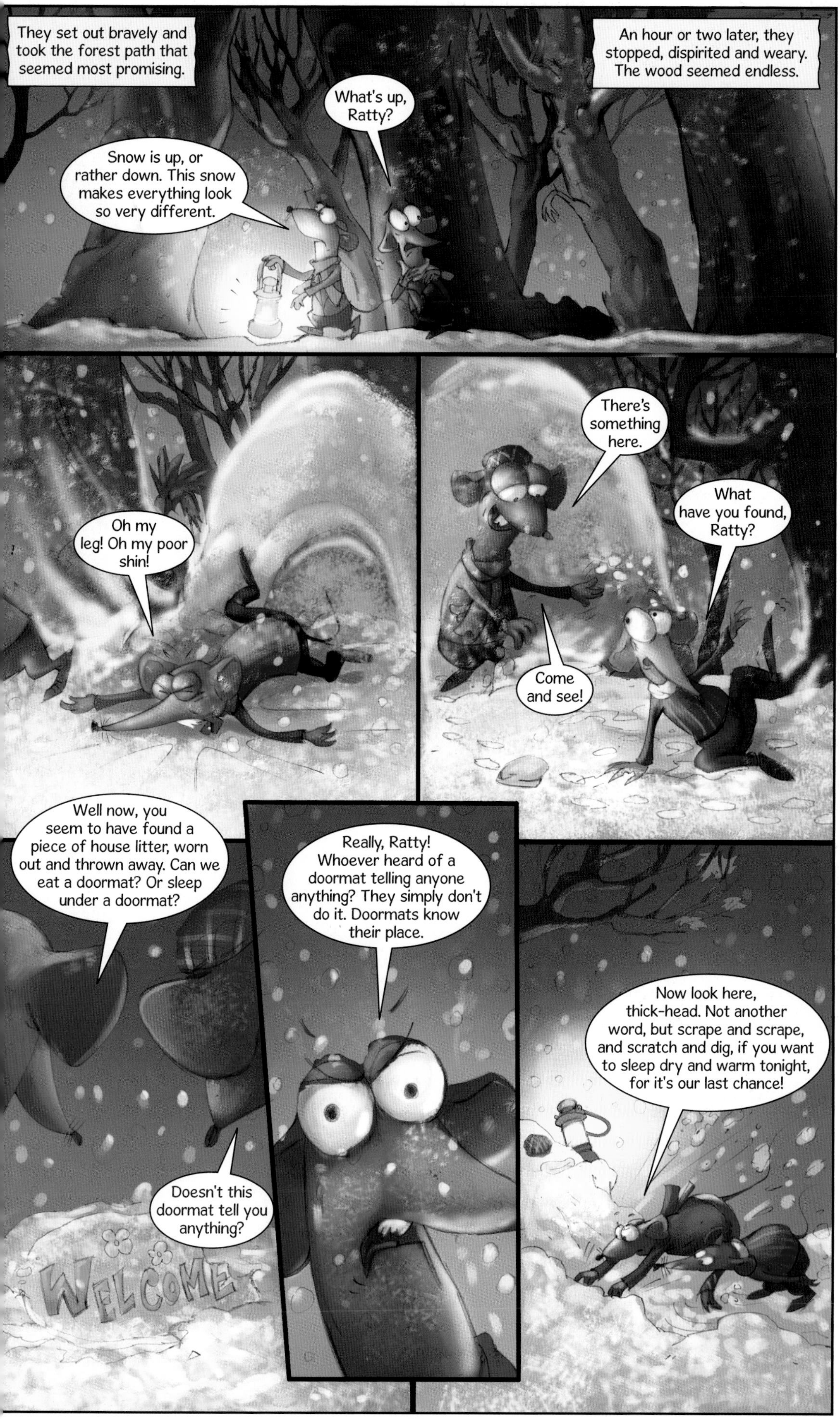
They set out bravely and took the forest path that seemed most promising.
What's up, Ratty?
Snow is up, or rather down. This snow makes everything look so very different.
An hour or two later, they stopped, dispirited and weary. The wood seemed endless.
Oh my leg! Oh my poor shin!
There's something here.
What have you found, Ratty?
Come and see!
Well now, you seem to have found a piece of house litter, worn out and thrown away. Can we eat a doormat? Or sleep under a doormat?
Doesn't this doormat tell you anything?
WELCOME
Really, Ratty! Whoever heard of a doormat telling anyone anything? They simply don't do it. Doormats know their place.
Now look here, thick-head. Not another word, but scrape and scrape, and scratch and dig, if you want to sleep dry and warm tonight, for it's our last chance!

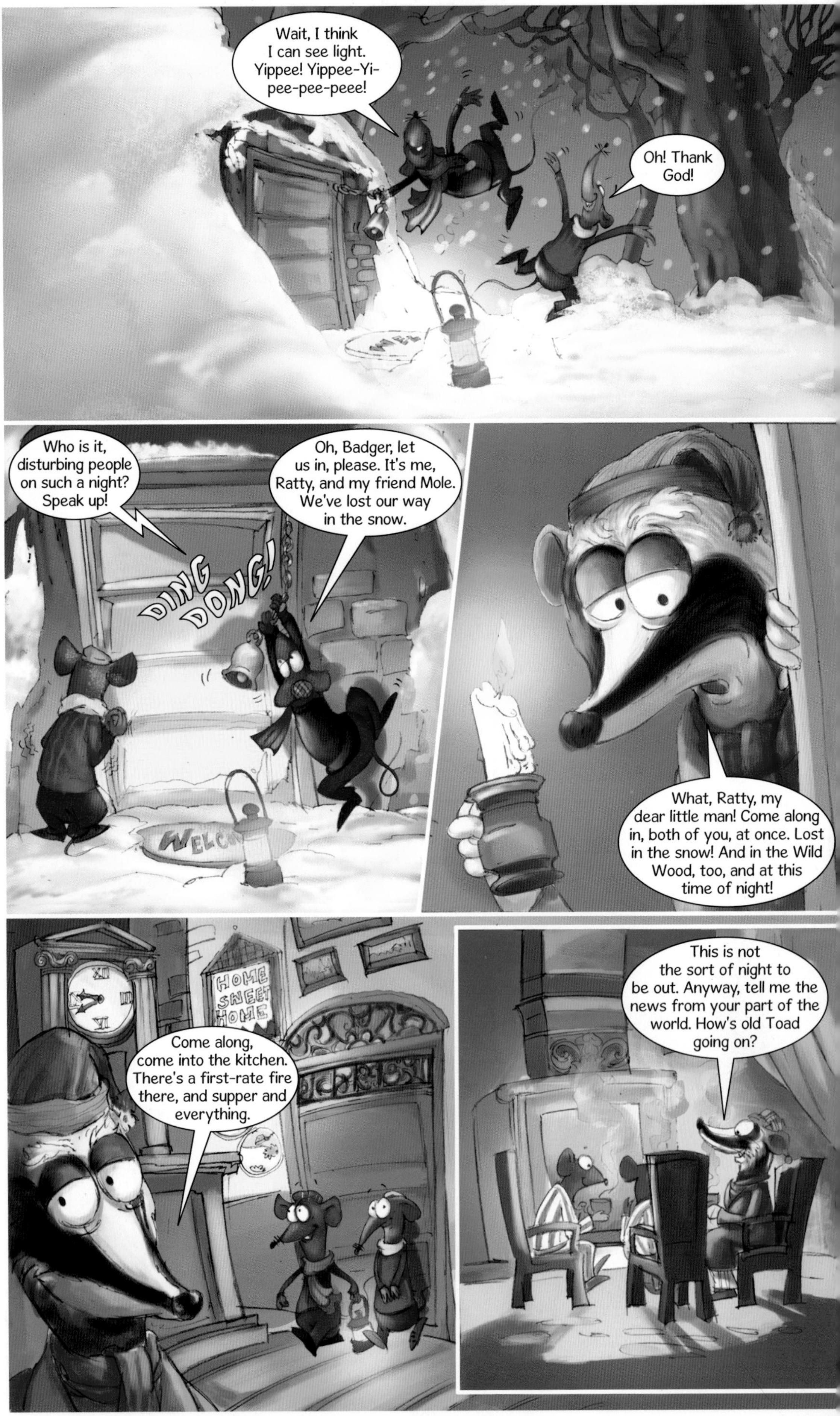

Wait, I think I can see light. Yippee! Yippee-Yi-pee-pee-peee!
Oh! Thank God!
Who is it, disturbing people on such a night? Speak up!
DING DONG!
Oh, Badger, let us in, please. It's me, Ratty, and my friend Mole. We've lost our way in the snow.
What, Ratty, my dear little man! Come along in, both of you, at once. Lost in the snow! And in the Wild Wood, too, and at this time of night!
HOME SWEET HOME
Come along, come into the kitchen. There's a first-rate fire there, and supper and everything.
This is not the sort of night to be out. Anyway, tell me the news from your part of the world. How's old Toad going on?

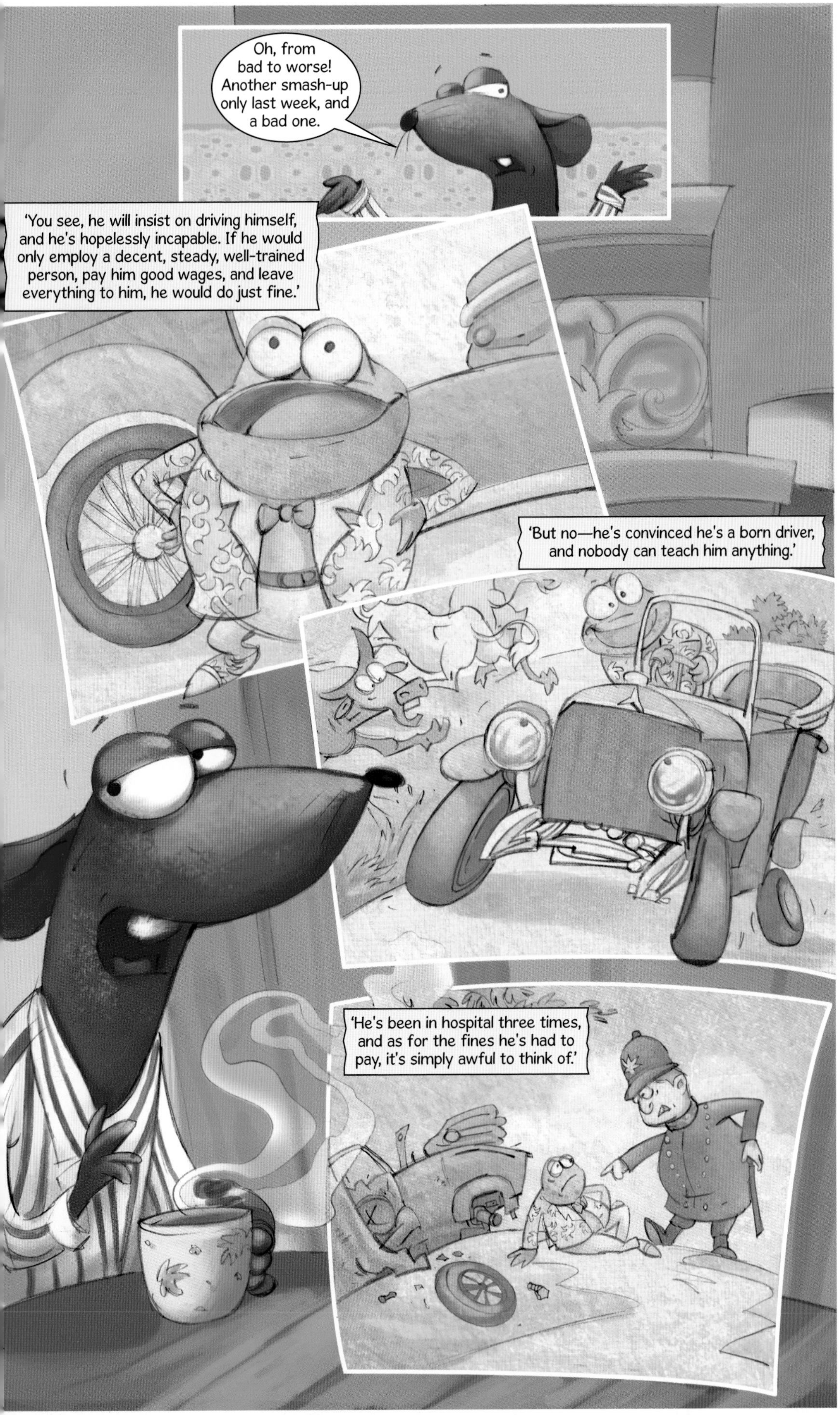
Oh, from bad to worse! Another smash-up only last week, and a bad one.
'You see, he will insist on driving himself, and he's hopelessly incapable. If he would only employ a decent, steady, well-trained person, pay him good wages, and leave everything to him, he would do just fine.'
'But no—he's convinced he's a born driver, and nobody can teach him anything.'
'He's been in hospital three times, and as for the fines he's had to pay, it's simply awful to think of.'

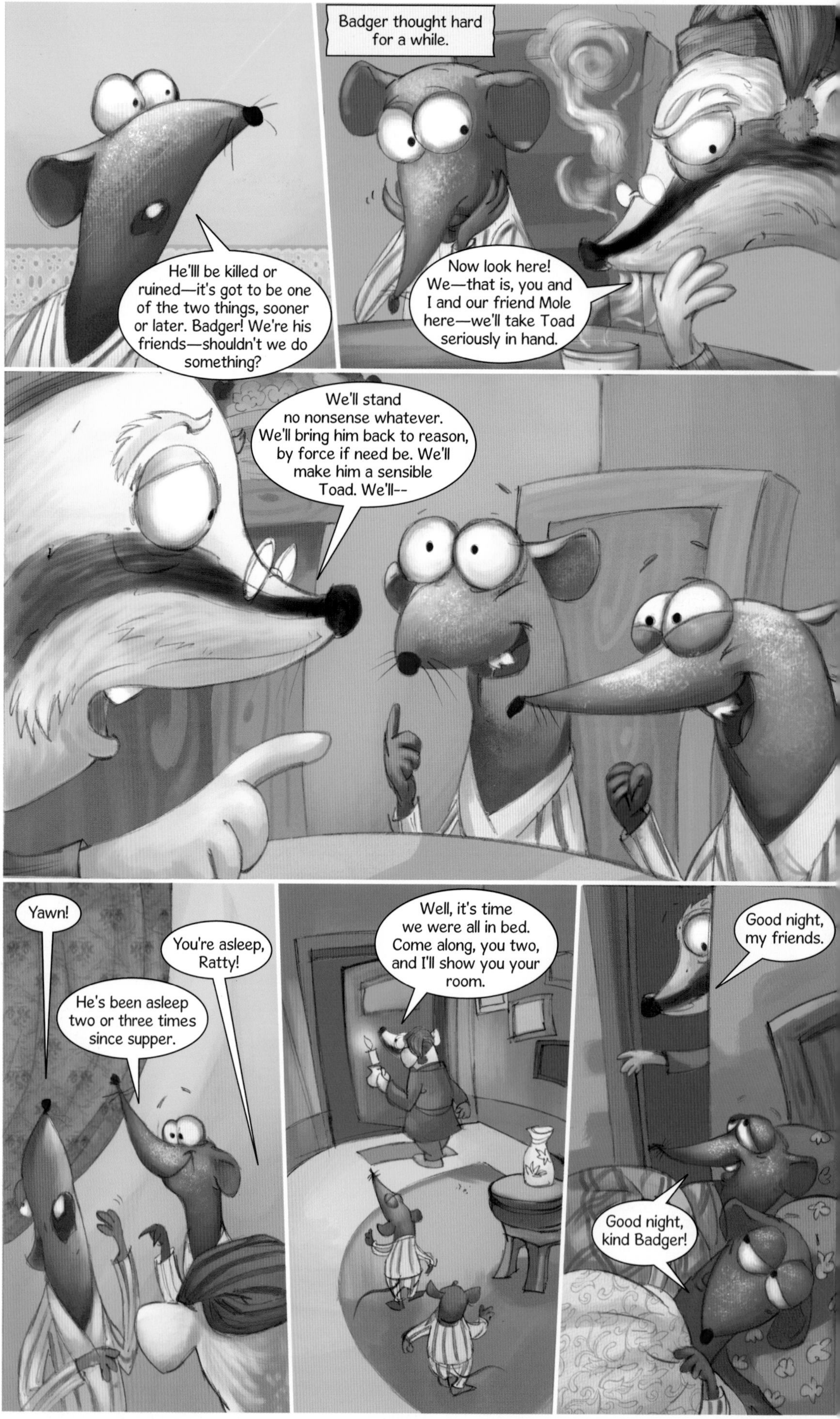
He'll be killed or ruined—it's got to be one of the two things, sooner or later. Badger! We're his friends—shouldn't we do something?
Badger thought hard for a while.
Now look here! We—that is, you and I and our friend Mole here—we'll take Toad seriously in hand.
We'll stand no nonsense whatever. We'll bring him back to reason, by force if need be. We'll make him a sensible Toad. We'll--
Yawn!
You're asleep, Ratty!
He's been asleep two or three times since supper.
Well, it's time we were all in bed. Come along, you two, and I'll show you your room.
Good night, my friends.
Good night, kind Badger!

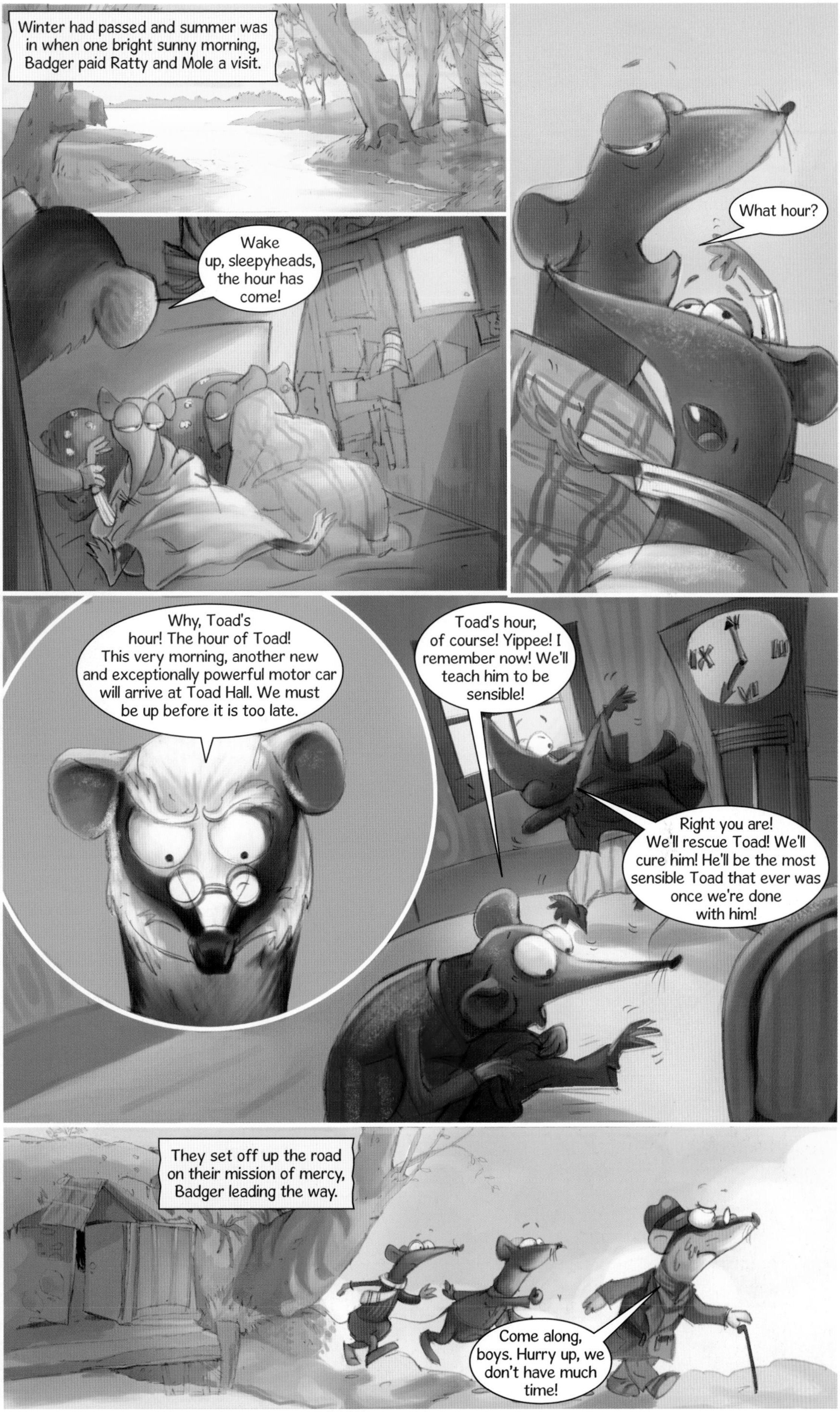
Winter had passed and summer was in when one bright sunny morning, Badger paid Ratty and Mole a visit.
Wake up, sleepyheads, the hour has come!
What hour?
Why, Toad's hour! The hour of Toad! This very morning, another new and exceptionally powerful motor car will arrive at Toad Hall. We must be up before it is too late.
Toad's hour, of course! Yippee! I remember now! We'll teach him to be sensible!
Right you are! We'll rescue Toad! We'll cure him! He'll be the most sensible Toad that ever was once we're done with him!
They set off up the road on their mission of mercy, Badger leading the way.
Come along, boys. Hurry up, we don't have much time!

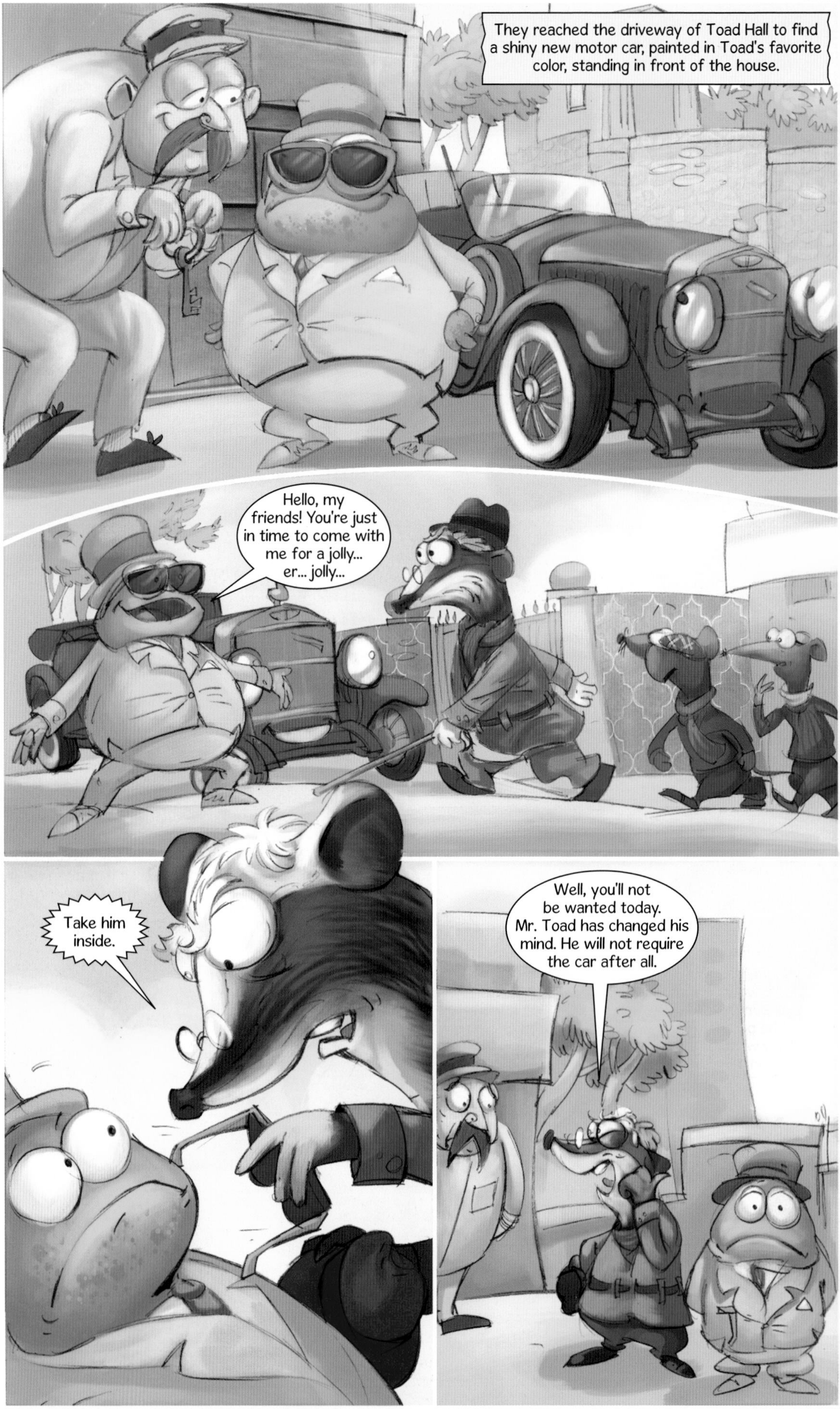
They reached the driveway of Toad Hall to find a shiny new motor car, painted in Toad's favorite color, standing in front of the house.
Hello, my friends! You're just in time to come with me for a jolly... er... jolly...
Take him inside.
Well, you'll not be wanted today. Mr. Toad has changed his mind. He will not require the car after all.

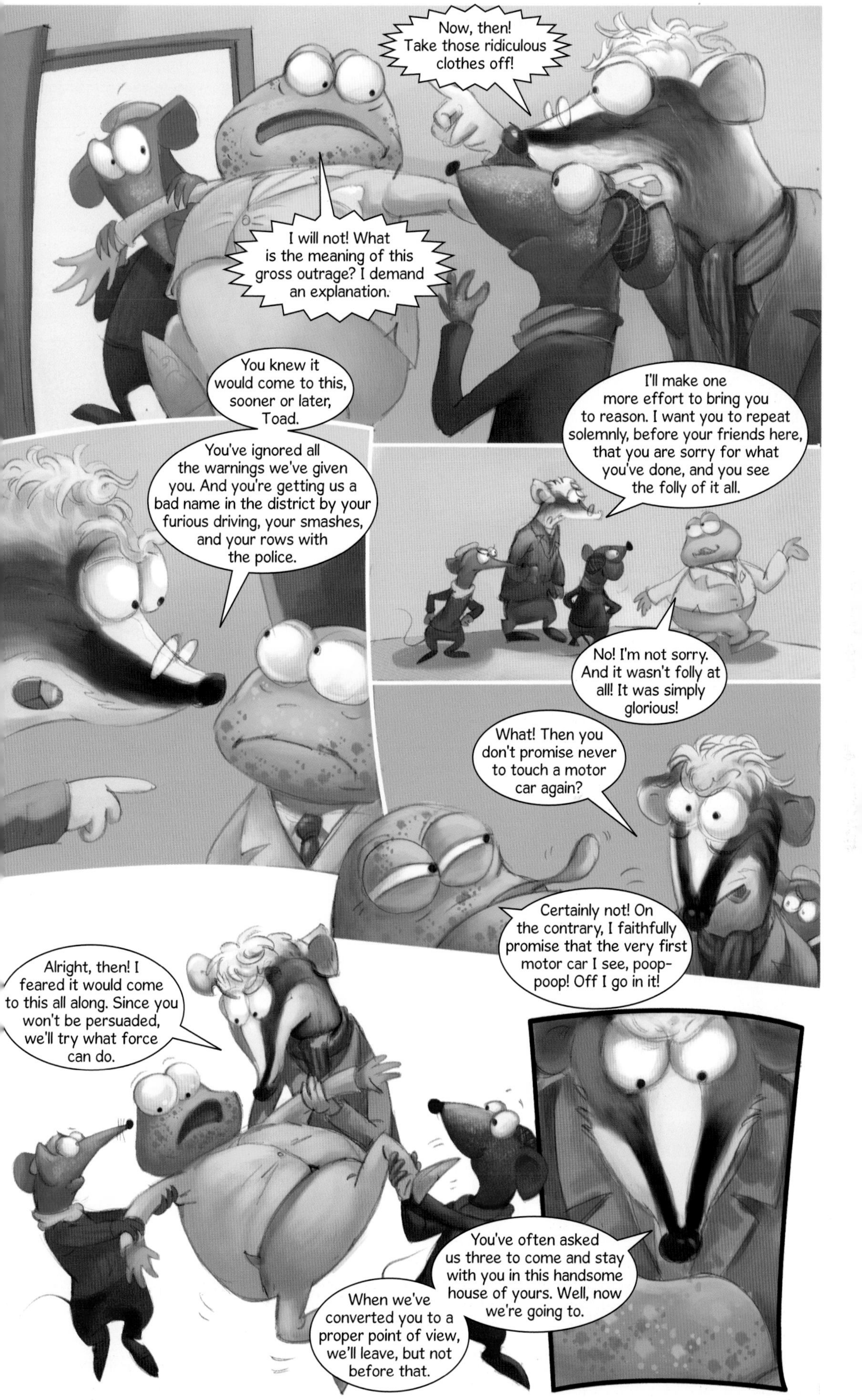
Now, then! Take those ridiculous clothes off!
I will not! What is the meaning of this gross outrage? I demand an explanation.
You knew it would come to this, sooner or later, Toad.
You've ignored all the warnings we've given you. And you're getting us a bad name in the district by your furious driving, your smashes, and your rows with the police.
I'll make one more effort to bring you to reason. I want you to repeat solemnly, before your friends here, that you are sorry for what you've done, and you see the folly of it all.
No! I'm not sorry. And it wasn't folly at all! It was simply glorious!
What! Then you don't promise never to touch a motor car again?
Certainly not! On the contrary, I faithfully promise that the very first motor car I see, poop-poop! Off I go in it!
Alright, then! I feared it would come to this all along. Since you won't be persuaded, we'll try what force can do.
You've often asked us three to come and stay with you in this handsome house of yours. Well, now we're going to.
When we've converted you to a proper point of view, we'll leave, but not before that.

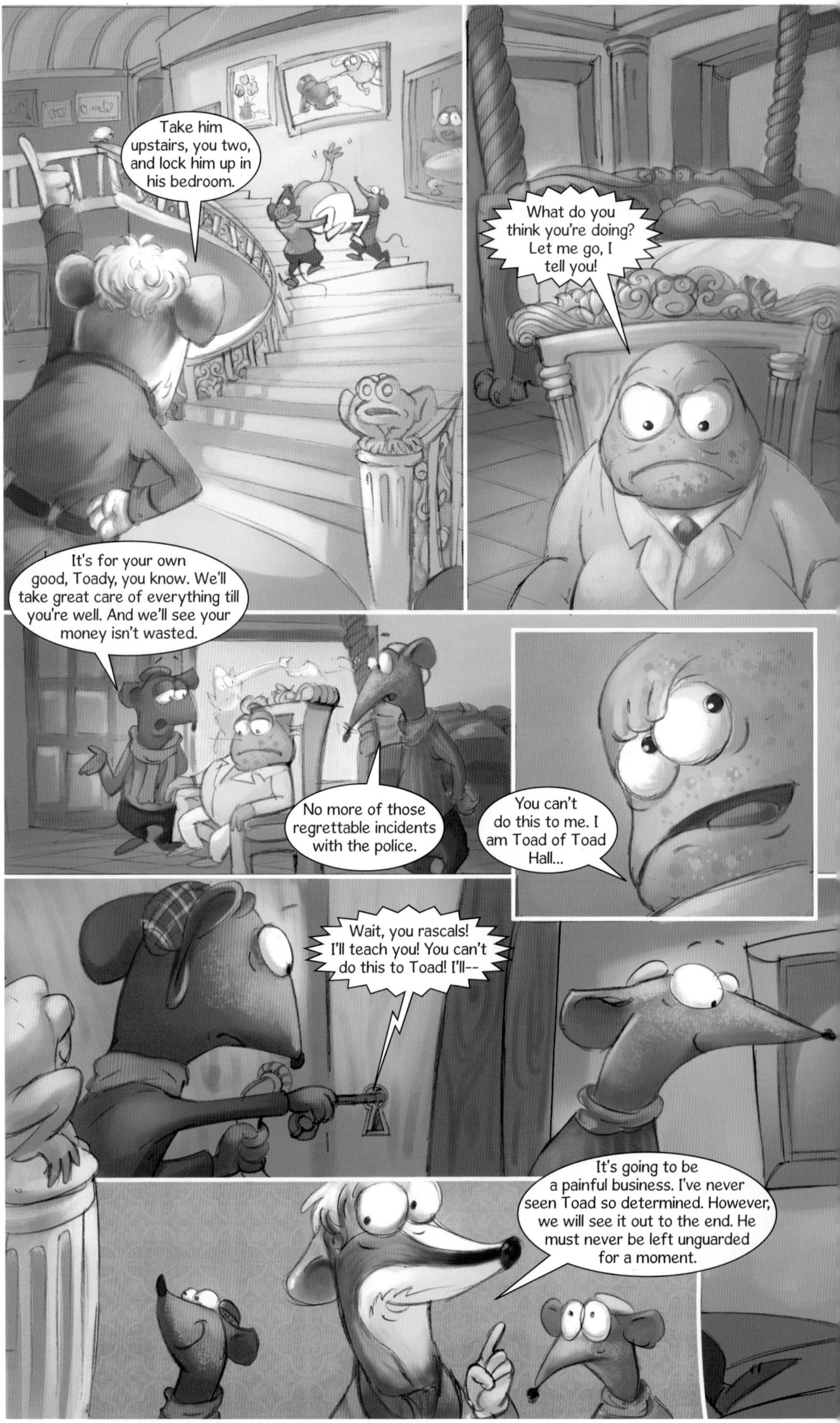
Take him upstairs, you two, and lock him up in his bedroom.
What do you think you're doing? Let me go, I tell you!
It's for your own good, Toady, you know. We'll take great care of everything till you're well. And we'll see your money isn't wasted.
No more of those regrettable incidents with the police.
You can't do this to me. I am Toad of Toad Hall...
Wait, you rascals! I'll teach you! You can't do this to Toad! I'll--
It's going to be a painful business. I've never seen Toad so determined. However, we will see it out to the end. He must never be left unguarded for a moment.

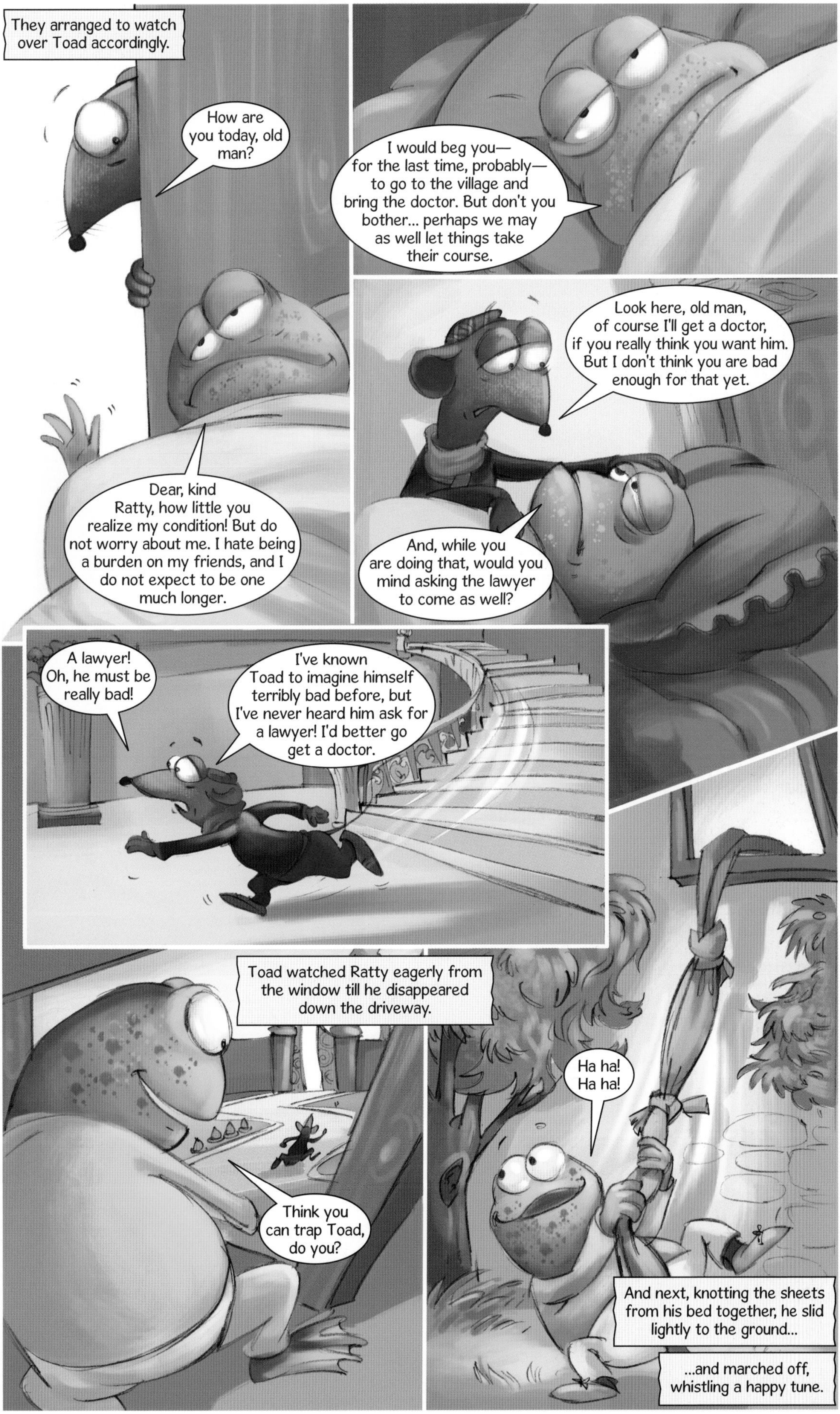

They arranged to watch over Toad accordingly.
How are you today, old man?
Dear, kind Ratty, how little you realize my condition! But do not worry about me. I hate being a burden on my friends, and I do not expect to be one much longer.
I would beg you— for the last time, probably— to go to the village and bring the doctor. But don't you bother... perhaps we may as well let things take their course.
Look here, old man, of course I'll get a doctor, if you really think you want him. But I don't think you are bad enough for that yet.
And, while you are doing that, would you mind asking the lawyer to come as well?
A lawyer! Oh, he must be really bad!
I've known Toad to imagine himself terribly bad before, but I've never heard him ask for a lawyer! I'd better go get a doctor.
Toad watched Ratty eagerly from the window till he disappeared down the driveway.
Think you can trap Toad, do you?
Ha ha! Ha ha!
And next, knotting the sheets from his bed together, he slid lightly to the ground...
...and marched off, whistling a happy tune.

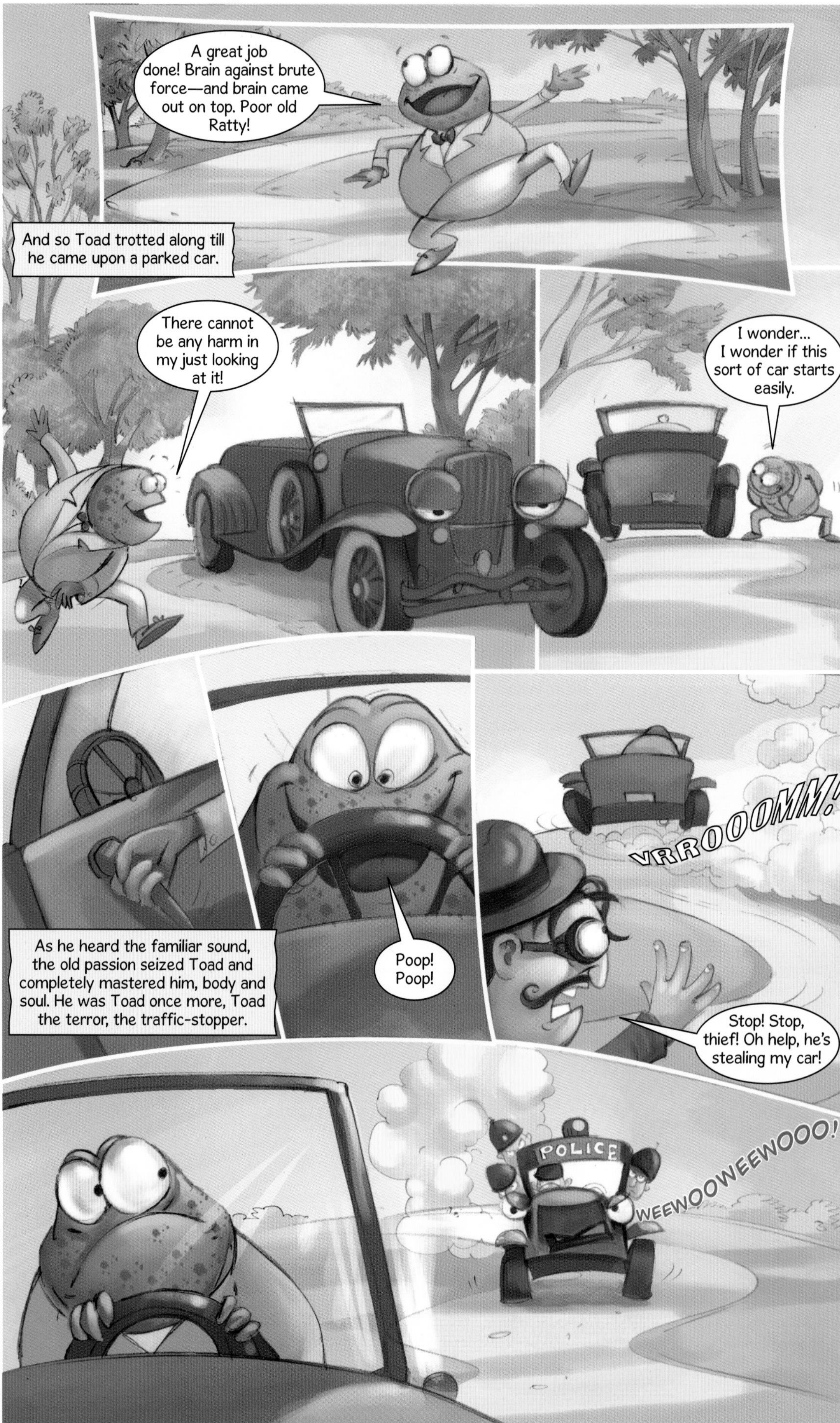
A great job done! Brain against brute force—and brain came out on top. Poor old Ratty!
And so Toad trotted along till he came upon a parked car.
There cannot be any harm in my just looking at it!
I wonder... I wonder if this sort of car starts easily.
As he heard the familiar sound, the old passion seized Toad and completely mastered him, body and soul. He was Toad once more, Toad the terror, the traffic-stopper.
Poop! Poop!
VRROOOOMM!
Stop! Stop, thief! Oh help, he's stealing my car!
POLICE
WEEWOOWEEWOOO!

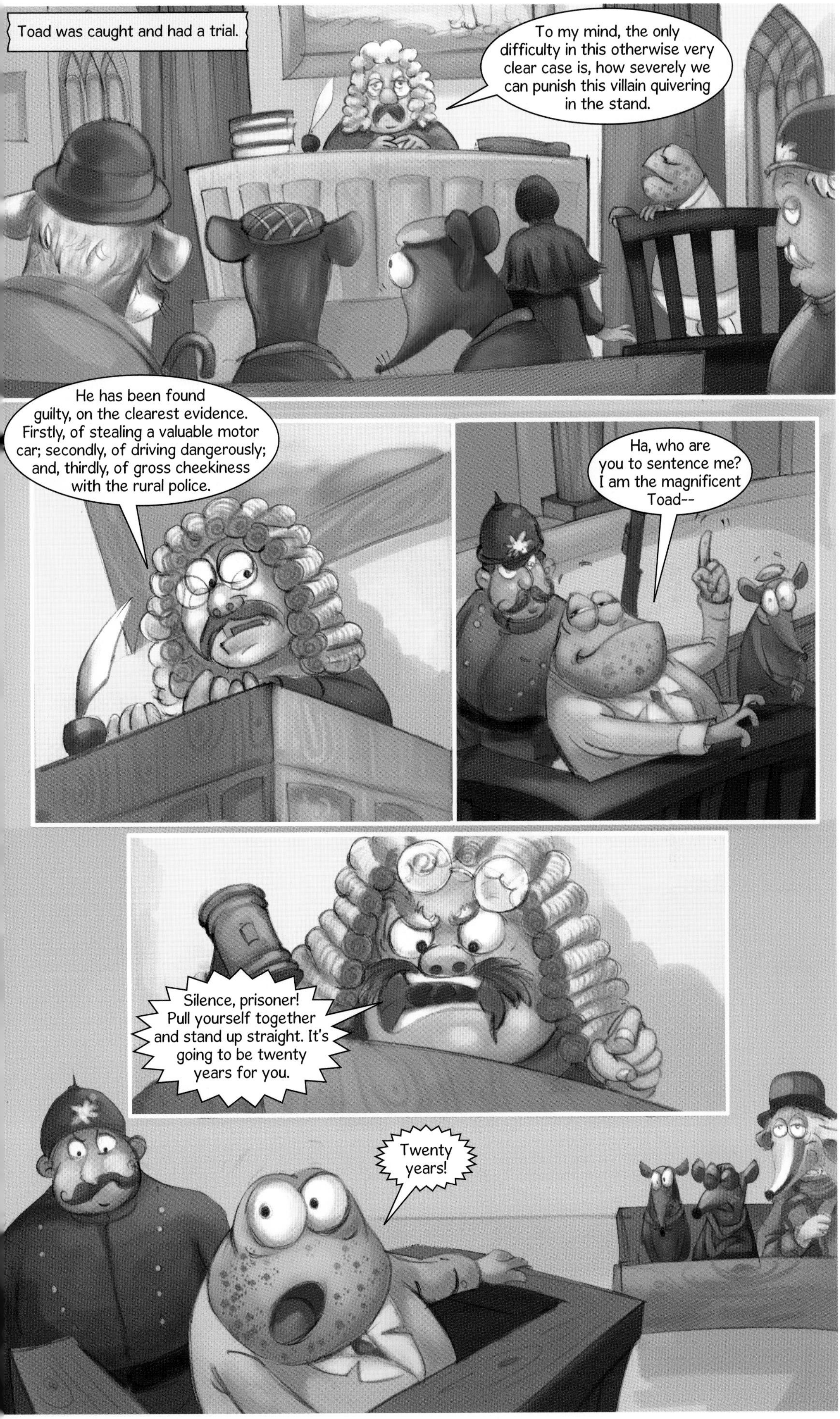
Toad was caught and had a trial.
To my mind, the only difficulty in this otherwise very clear case is, how severely we can punish this villain quivering in the stand.
He has been found guilty, on the clearest evidence. Firstly, of stealing a valuable motor car; secondly, of driving dangerously; and, thirdly, of gross cheekiness with the rural police.
Ha, who are you to sentence me? I am the magnificent Toad--
Silence, prisoner! Pull yourself together and stand up straight. It's going to be twenty years for you.
Twenty years!

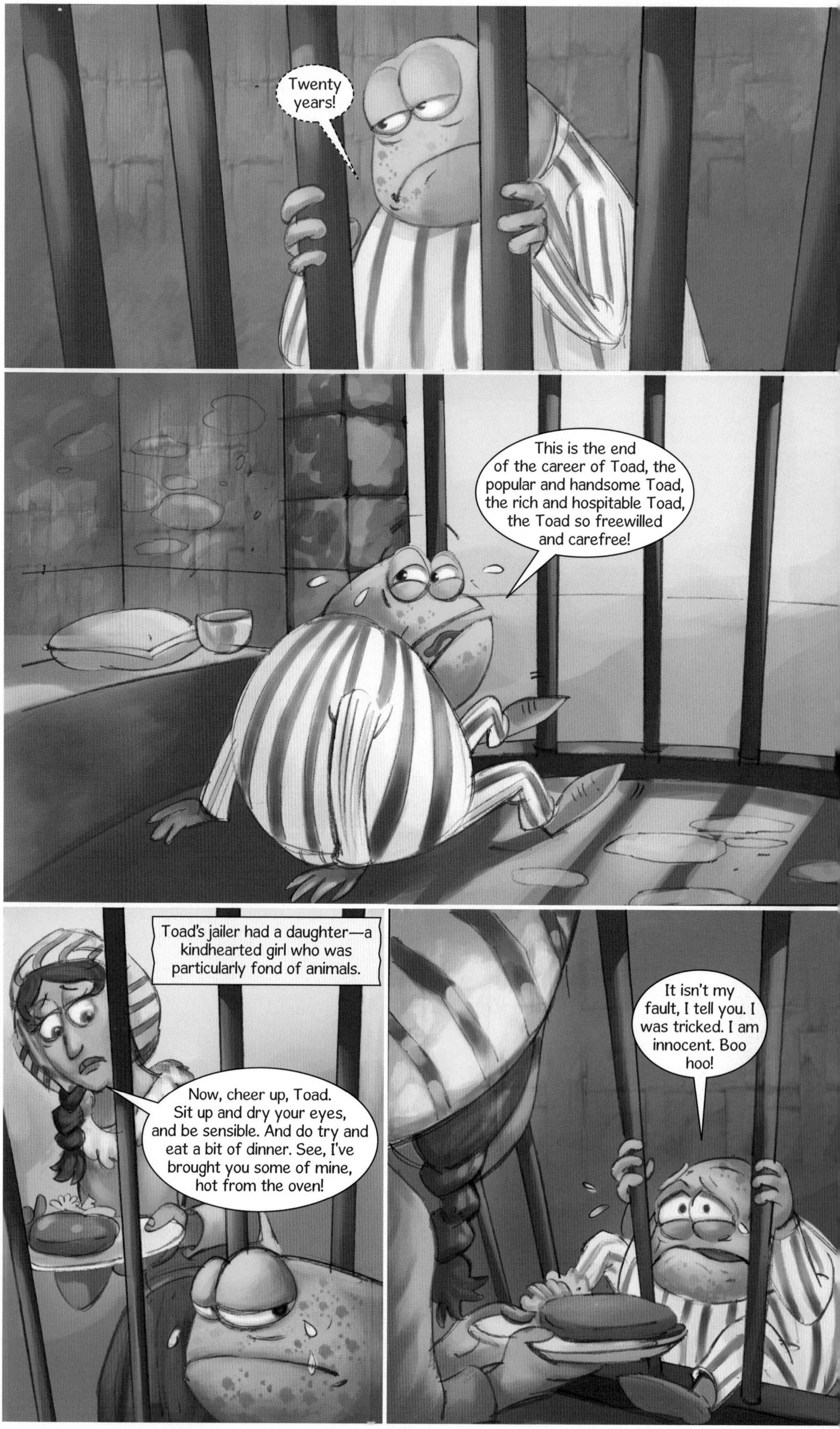
Twenty years!
This is the end of the career of Toad, the popular and handsome Toad, the rich and hospitable Toad, the Toad so freewilled and carefree!
Toad's jailer had a daughter—a kindhearted girl who was particularly fond of animals.
Now, cheer up, Toad. Sit up and dry your eyes, and be sensible. And do try and eat a bit of dinner. See, I've brought you some of mine, hot from the oven!
It isn't my fault, I tell you. I was tricked. I am innocent. Boo hoo!

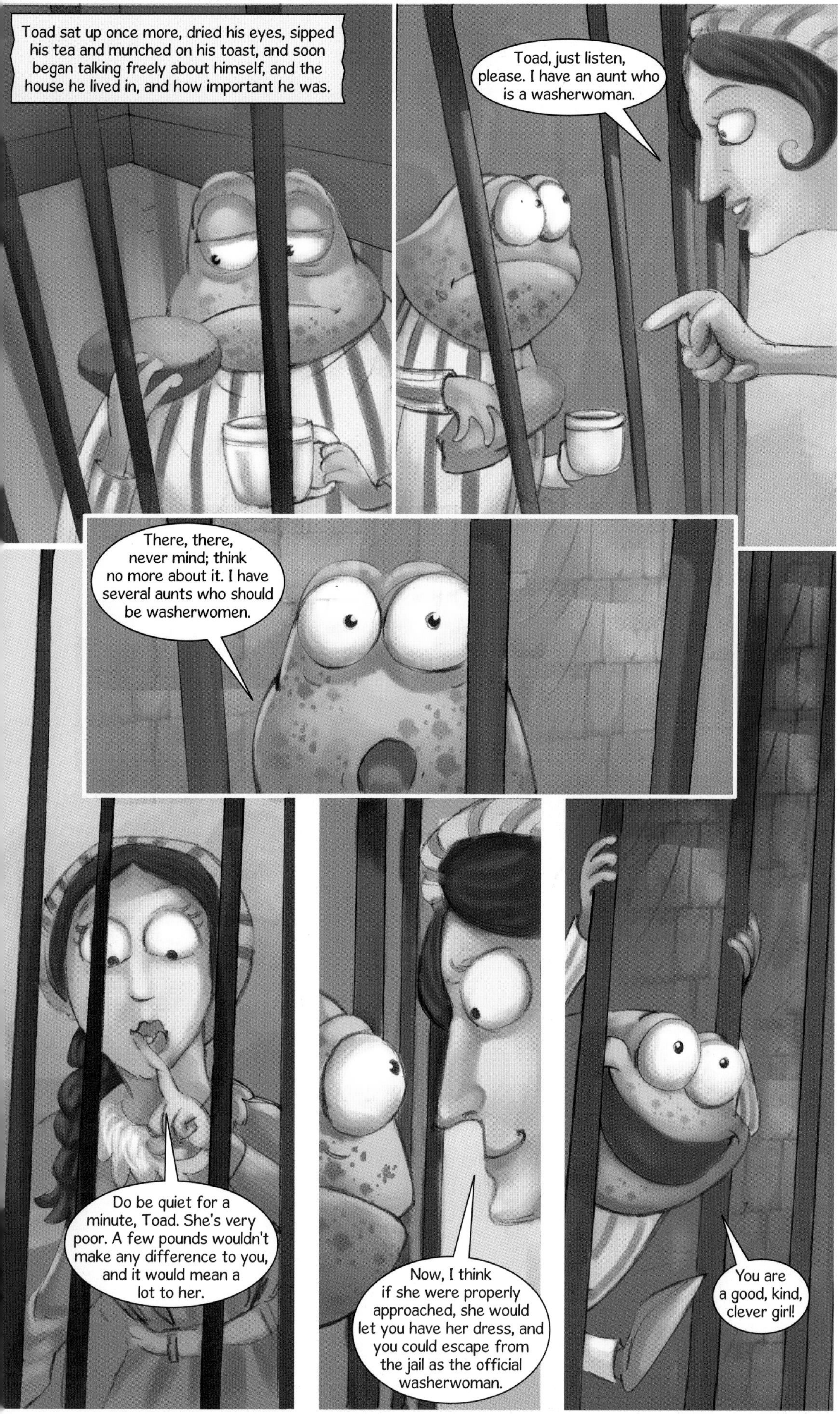

Toad sat up once more, dried his eyes, sipped his tea and munched on his toast, and soon began talking freely about himself, and the house he lived in, and how important he was.
Toad, just listen, please. I have an aunt who is a washerwoman.
There, there, never mind; think no more about it. I have several aunts who should be washerwomen.
Do be quiet for a minute, Toad. She's very poor. A few pounds wouldn't make any difference to you, and it would mean a lot to her.
Now, I think if she were properly approached, she would let you have her dress, and you could escape from the jail as the official washerwoman.
You are a good, kind, clever girl!

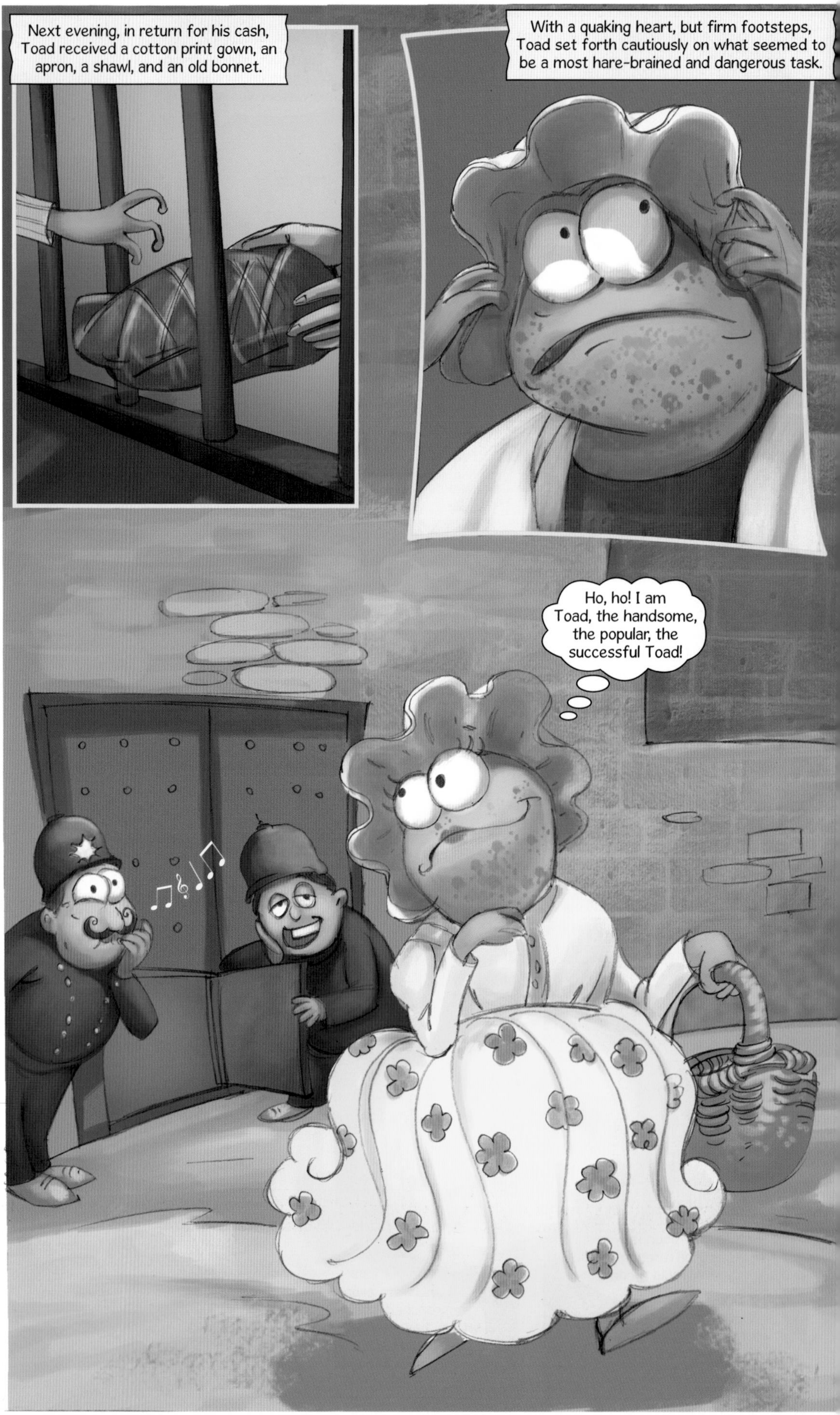
Next evening, in return for his cash, Toad received a cotton print gown, an apron, a shawl, and an old bonnet.
With a quaking heart, but firm footsteps, Toad set forth cautiously on what seemed to be a most hare-brained and dangerous task.
Ho, ho! I am Toad, the handsome, the popular, the successful Toad!

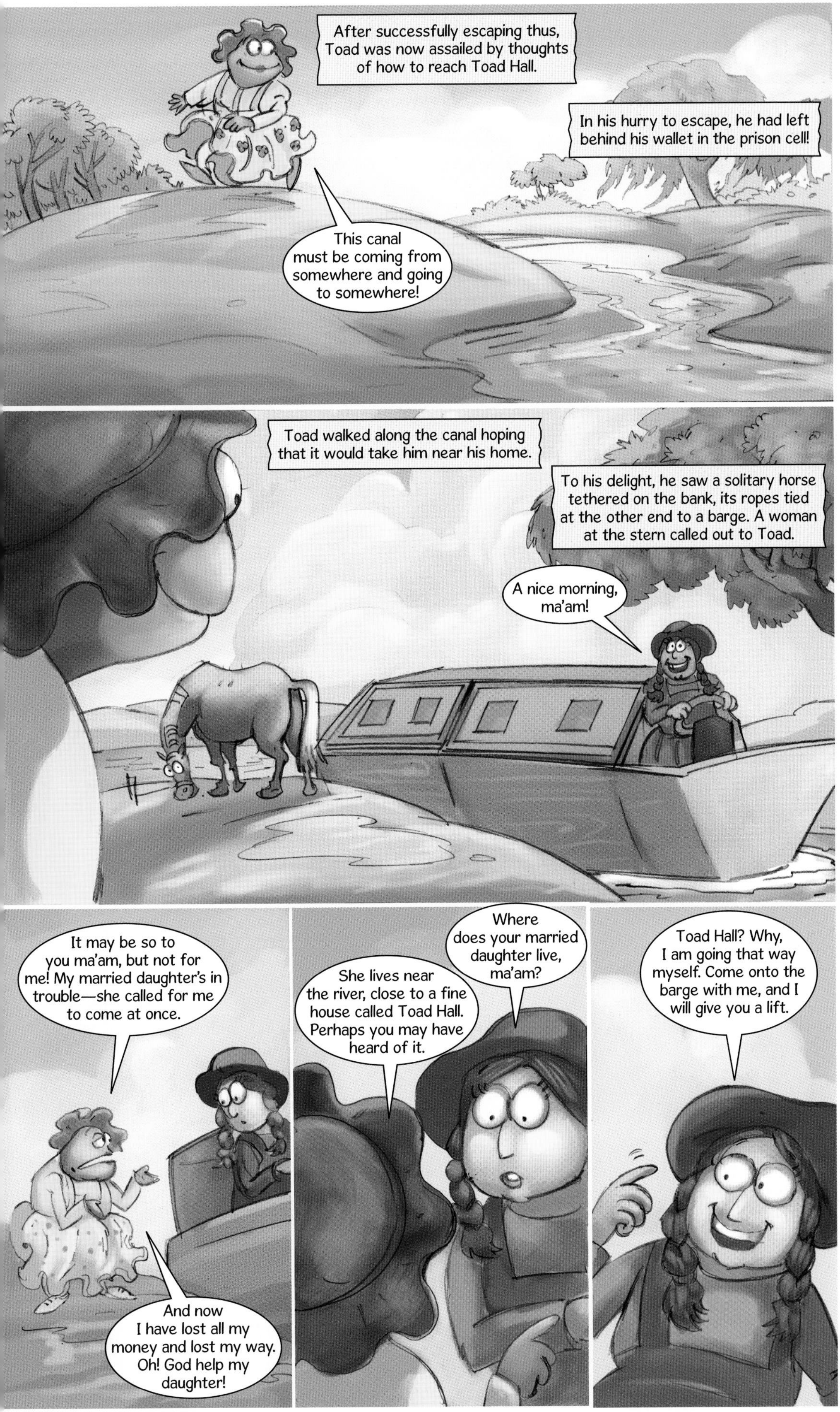
After successfully escaping thus, Toad was now assailed by thoughts of how to reach Toad Hall.
In his hurry to escape, he had left behind his wallet in the prison cell!
This canal must be coming from somewhere and going to somewhere!
Toad walked along the canal hoping that it would take him near his home.
To his delight, he saw a solitary horse tethered on the bank, its ropes tied at the other end to a barge. A woman at the stern called out to Toad.
A nice morning, ma'am!
It may be so to you ma'am, but not for me! My married daughter's in trouble—she called for me to come at once.
And now I have lost all my money and lost my way. Oh! God help my daughter!
Where does your married daughter live, ma'am?
She lives near the river, close to a fine house called Toad Hall. Perhaps you may have heard of it.
Toad Hall? Why, I am going that way myself. Come onto the barge with me, and I will give you a lift.

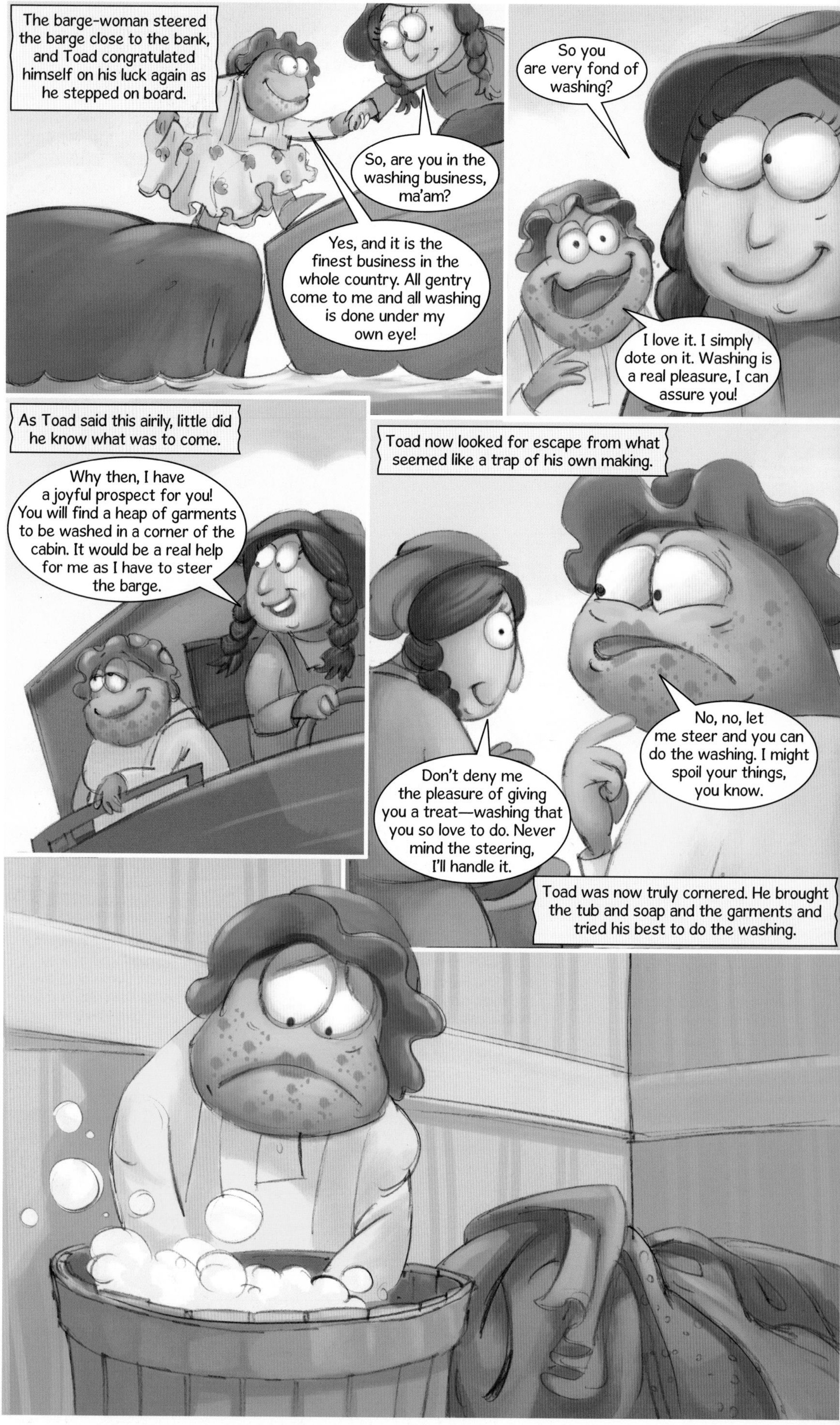
The barge-woman steered the barge close to the bank, and Toad congratulated himself on his luck again as he stepped on board.
So, are you in the washing business, ma'am?
Yes, and it is the finest business in the whole country. All gentry come to me and all washing is done under my own eye!
So you are very fond of washing?
I love it. I simply dote on it. Washing is a real pleasure, I can assure you!
As Toad said this airily, little did he know what was to come.
Why then, I have a joyful prospect for you! You will find a heap of garments to be washed in a corner of the cabin. It would be a real help for me as I have to steer the barge.
Toad now looked for escape from what seemed like a trap of his own making.
No, no, let me steer and you can do the washing. I might spoil your things, you know.
Don't deny me the pleasure of giving you a treat—washing that you so love to do. Never mind the steering, I'll handle it.
Toad was now truly cornered. He brought the tub and soap and the garments and tried his best to do the washing.

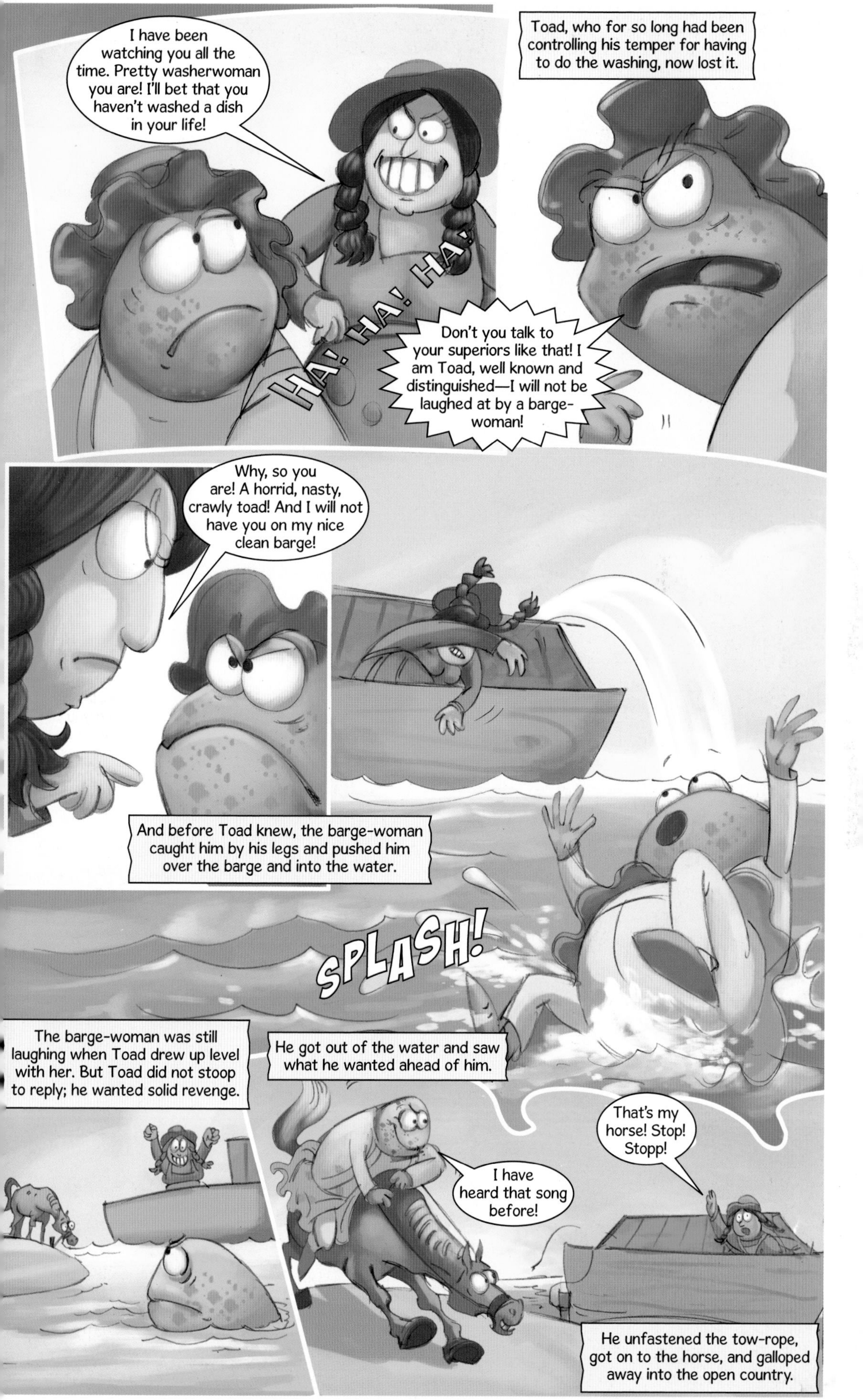
I have been watching you all the time. Pretty washerwoman you are! I'll bet that you haven't washed a dish in your life!
HA! HA! HA!
Toad, who for so long had been controlling his temper for having to do the washing, now lost it.
Don't you talk to your superiors like that! I am Toad, well known and distinguished—I will not be laughed at by a barge-woman!
Why, so you are! A horrid, nasty, crawly toad! And I will not have you on my nice clean barge!
And before Toad knew, the barge-woman caught him by his legs and pushed him over the barge and into the water.
SPLASH!
The barge-woman was still laughing when Toad drew up level with her. But Toad did not stoop to reply; he wanted solid revenge.
He got out of the water and saw what he wanted ahead of him.
I have heard that song before!
That's my horse! Stop! Stopp!
He unfastened the tow-rope, got on to the horse, and galloped away into the open country.

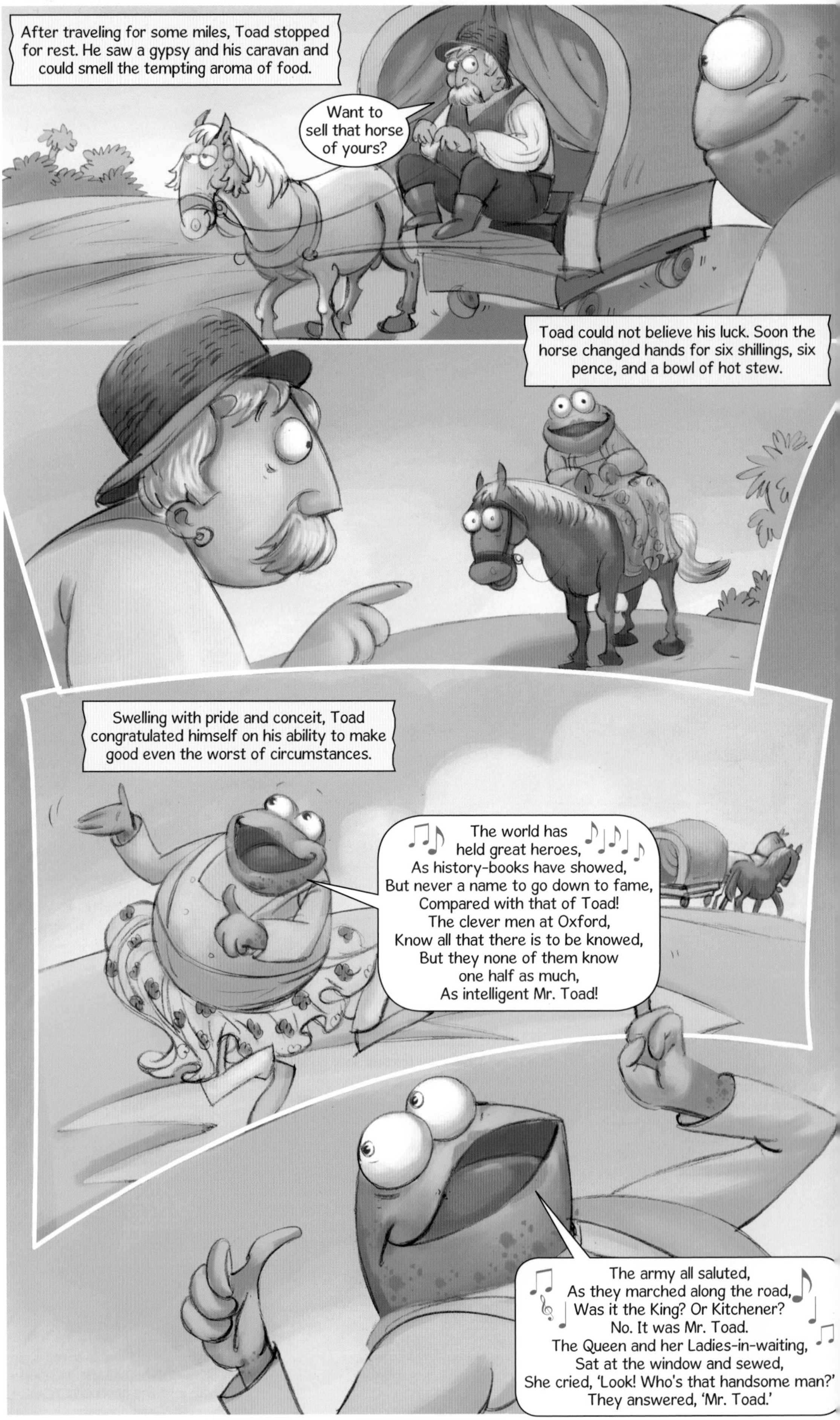
After traveling for some miles, Toad stopped for rest. He saw a gypsy and his caravan and could smell the tempting aroma of food.
Want to sell that horse of yours?
Toad could not believe his luck. Soon the horse changed hands for six shillings, six pence, and a bowl of hot stew.
Swelling with pride and conceit, Toad congratulated himself on his ability to make good even the worst of circumstances.
The world has held great heroes, As history-books have showed, But never a name to go down to fame, Compared with that of Toad! The clever men at Oxford, Know all that there is to be knowed, But they none of them know one half as much, As intelligent Mr. Toad!
The army all saluted, As they marched along the road, Was it the King? Or Kitchener? No. It was Mr. Toad. The Queen and her Ladies-in-waiting, Sat at the window and sewed, She cried, 'Look! Who's that handsome man?' They answered, 'Mr. Toad.'

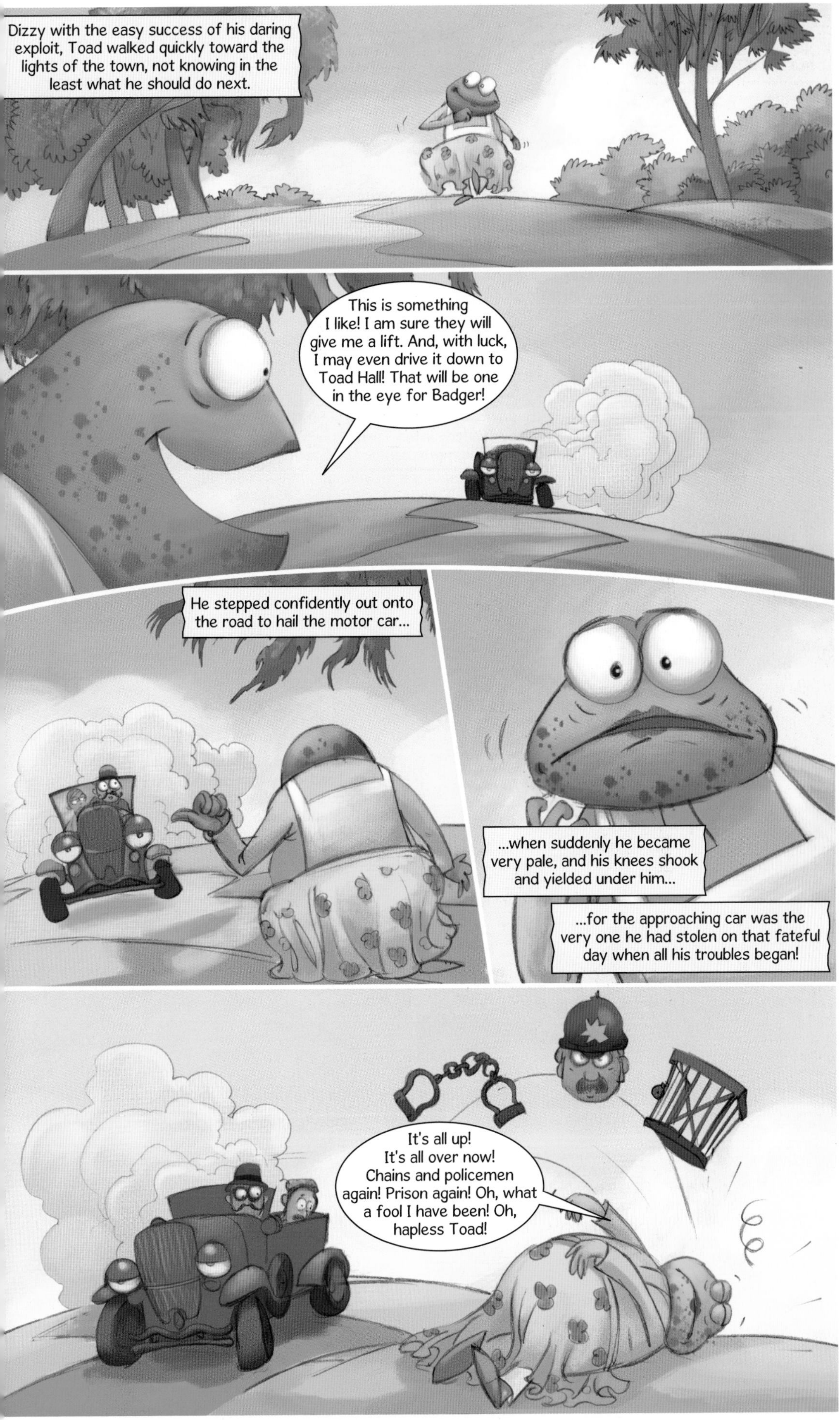
Dizzy with the easy success of his daring exploit, Toad walked quickly toward the lights of the town, not knowing in the least what he should do next.
This is something I like! I am sure they will give me a lift. And, with luck, I may even drive it down to Toad Hall! That will be one in the eye for Badger!
He stepped confidently out onto the road to hail the motor car...
...when suddenly he became very pale, and his knees shook and yielded under him...
...for the approaching car was the very one he had stolen on that fateful day when all his troubles began!
It's all up! It's all over now! Chains and policemen again! Prison again! Oh, what a fool I have been! Oh, hapless Toad!

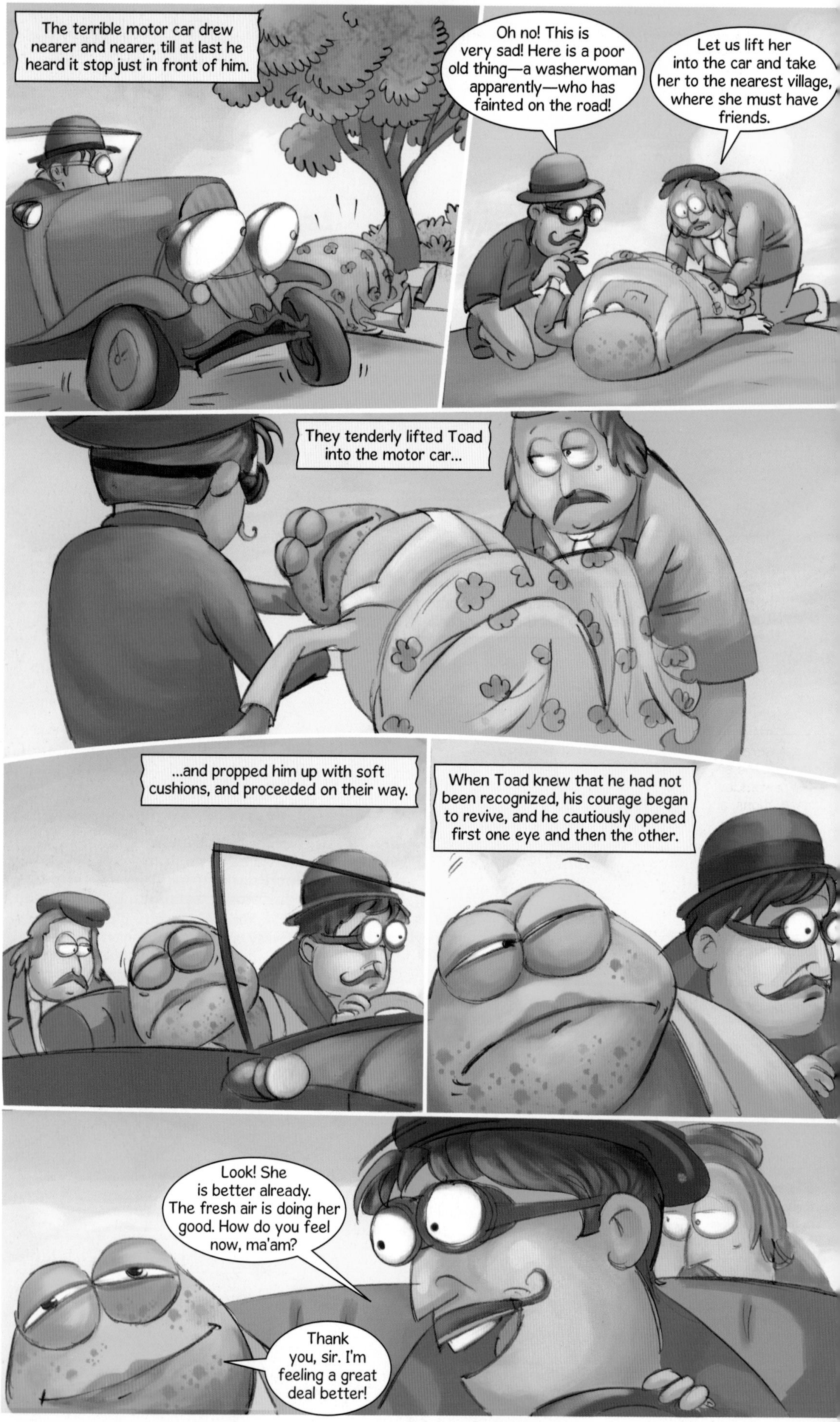
The terrible motor car drew nearer and nearer, till at last he heard it stop just in front of him.
Oh no! This is very sad! Here is a poor old thing—a washerwoman apparently—who has fainted on the road!
Let us lift her into the car and take her to the nearest village, where she must have friends.
They tenderly lifted Toad into the motor car...
...and propped him up with soft cushions, and proceeded on their way.
When Toad knew that he had not been recognized, his courage began to revive, and he cautiously opened first one eye and then the other.
Look! She is better already. The fresh air is doing her good. How do you feel now, ma'am?
Thank you, sir. I'm feeling a great deal better!

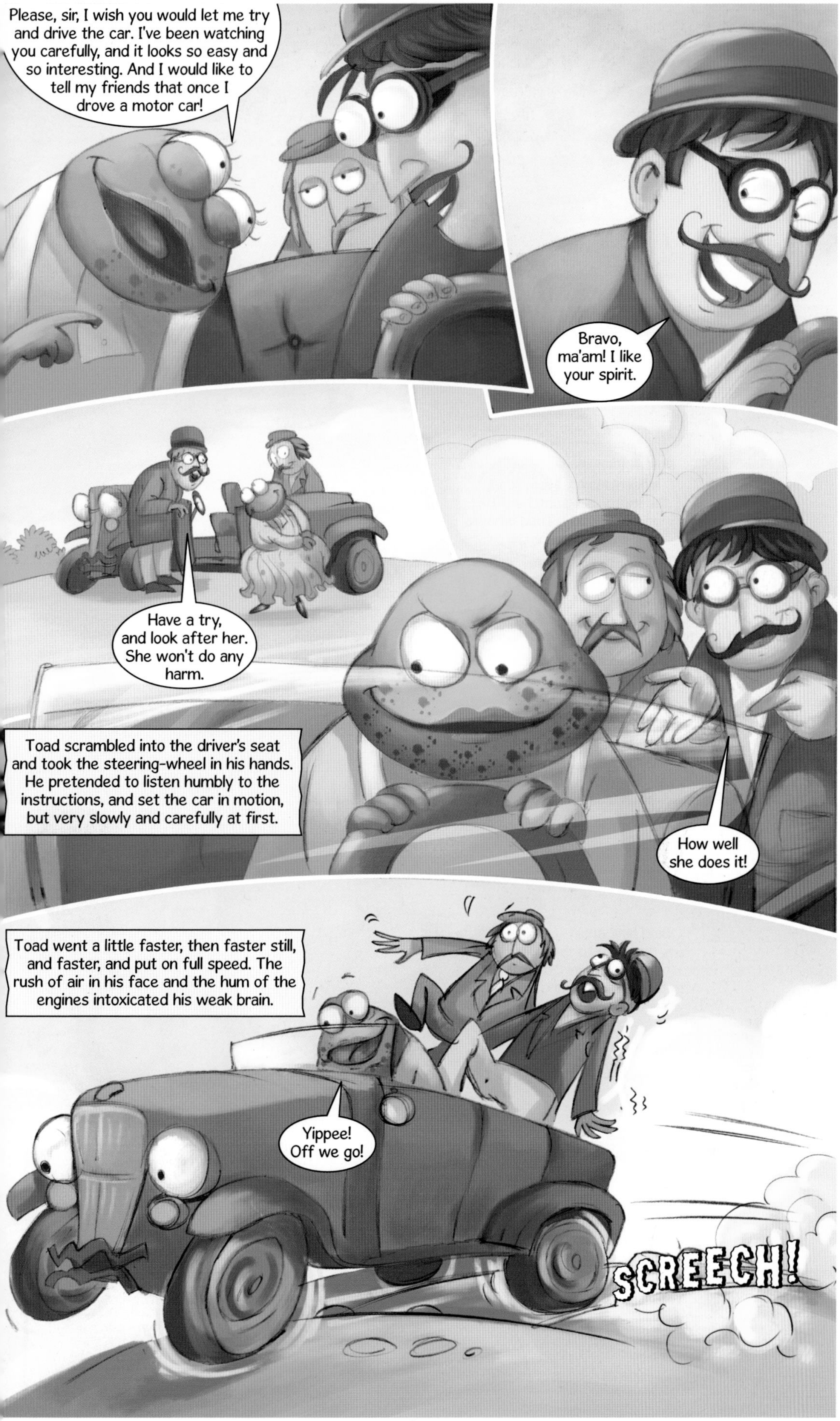
Please, sir, I wish you would let me try and drive the car. I've been watching you carefully, and it looks so easy and so interesting. And I would like to tell my friends that once I drove a motor car!
Bravo, ma'am! I like your spirit.
Have a try, and look after her. She won't do any harm.
Toad scrambled into the driver's seat and took the steering-wheel in his hands. He pretended to listen humbly to the instructions, and set the car in motion, but very slowly and carefully at first.
How well she does it!
Toad went a little faster, then faster still, and faster, and put on full speed. The rush of air in his face and the hum of the engines intoxicated his weak brain.
Yippee! Off we go!
SCREECH!

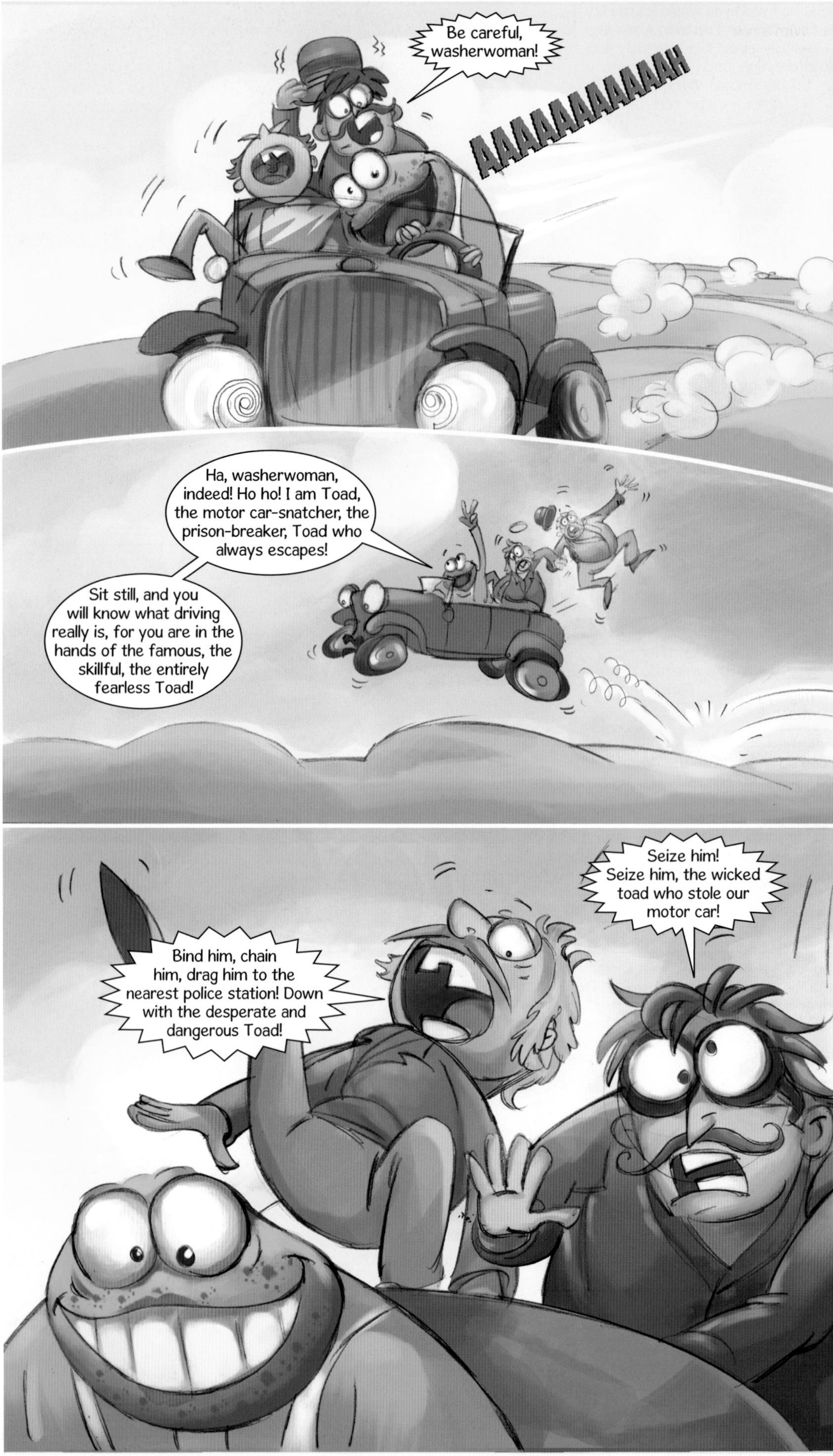
Be careful, washerwoman!
AAAAAAAAAAAH
Ha, washerwoman, indeed! Ho ho! I am Toad, the motor car-snatcher, the prison-breaker, Toad who always escapes!
Sit still, and you will know what driving really is, for you are in the hands of the famous, the skillful, the entirely fearless Toad!
Seize him! Seize him, the wicked toad who stole our motor car!
Bind him, chain him, drag him to the nearest police station! Down with the desperate and dangerous Toad!

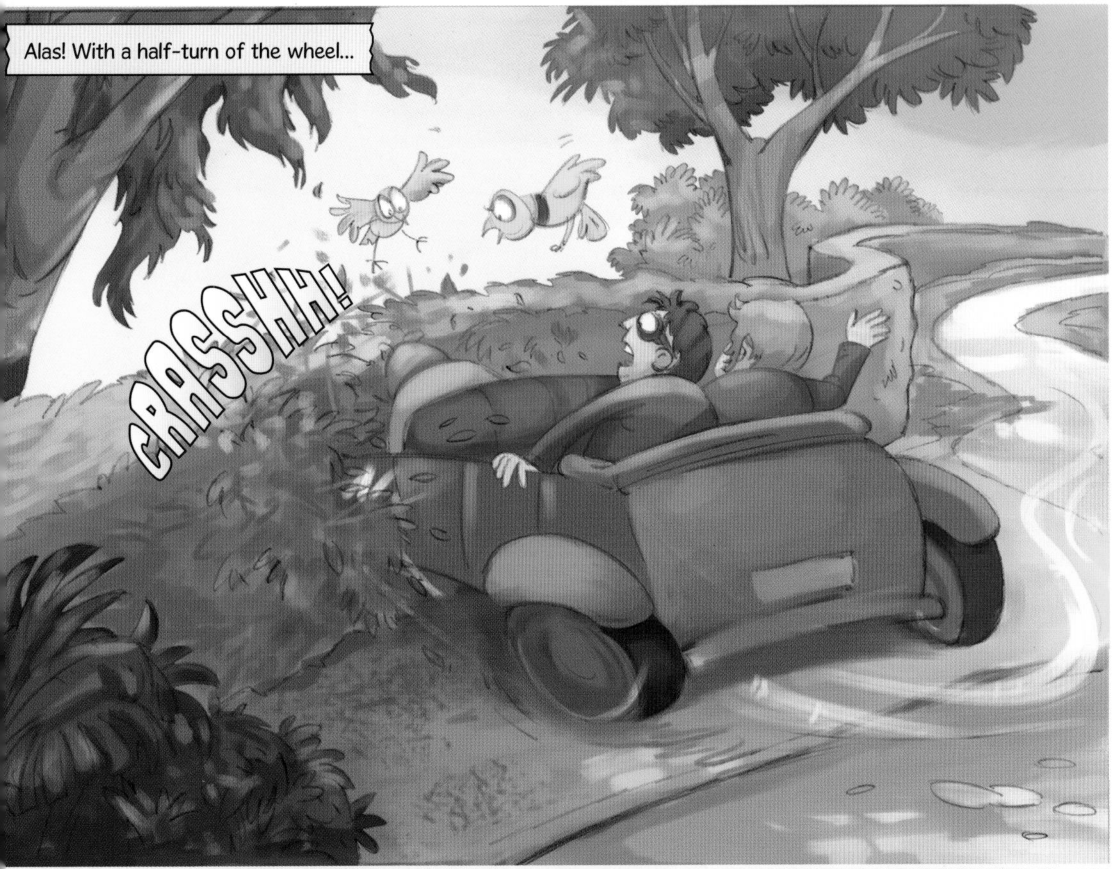
Alas! With a half-turn of the wheel...
CRASSHH!

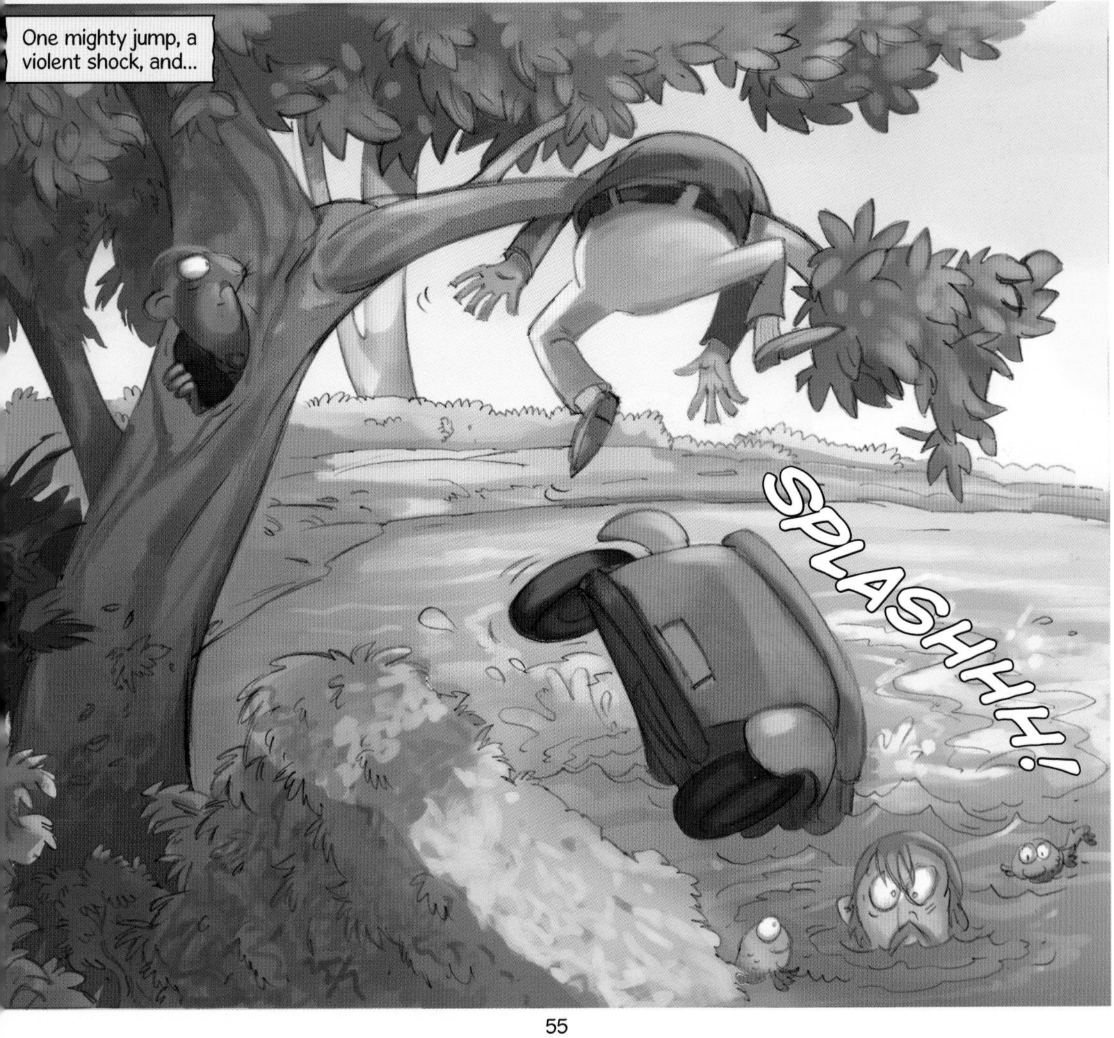
One mighty jump, a violent shock, and...
SPLASHHH!

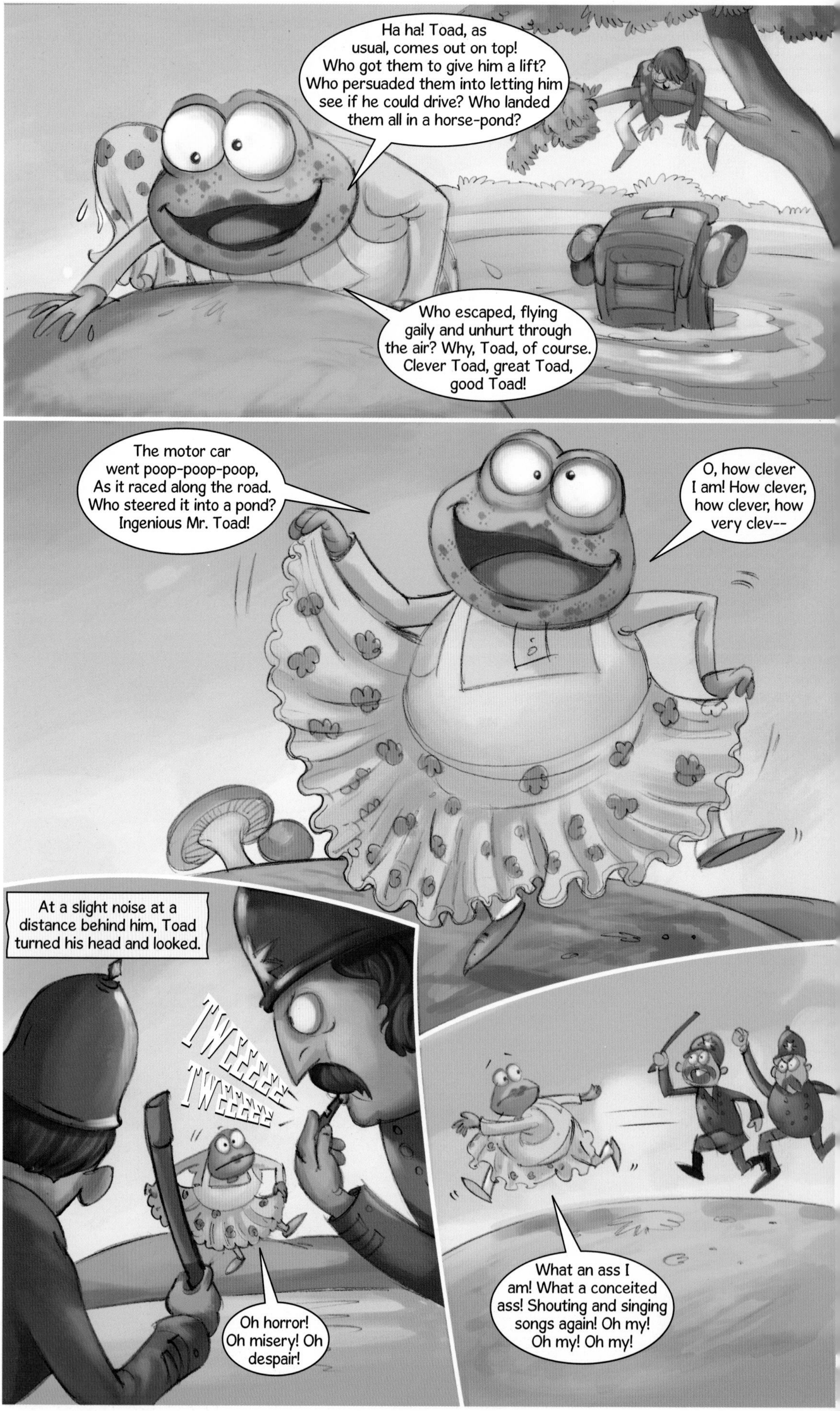
Ha ha! Toad, as usual, comes out on top! Who got them to give him a lift? Who persuaded them into letting him see if he could drive? Who landed them all in a horse-pond?
Who escaped, flying gaily and unhurt through the air? Why, Toad, of course. Clever Toad, great Toad, good Toad!
The motor car went poop-poop-poop, As it raced along the road. Who steered it into a pond? Ingenious Mr. Toad!
O, how clever I am! How clever, how clever, how very clev--
At a slight noise at a distance behind him, Toad turned his head and looked.
TWEEEEEE TWEEEEEE
Oh horror! Oh misery! Oh despair!
What an ass I am! What a conceited ass! Shouting and singing songs again! Oh my! Oh my! Oh my!

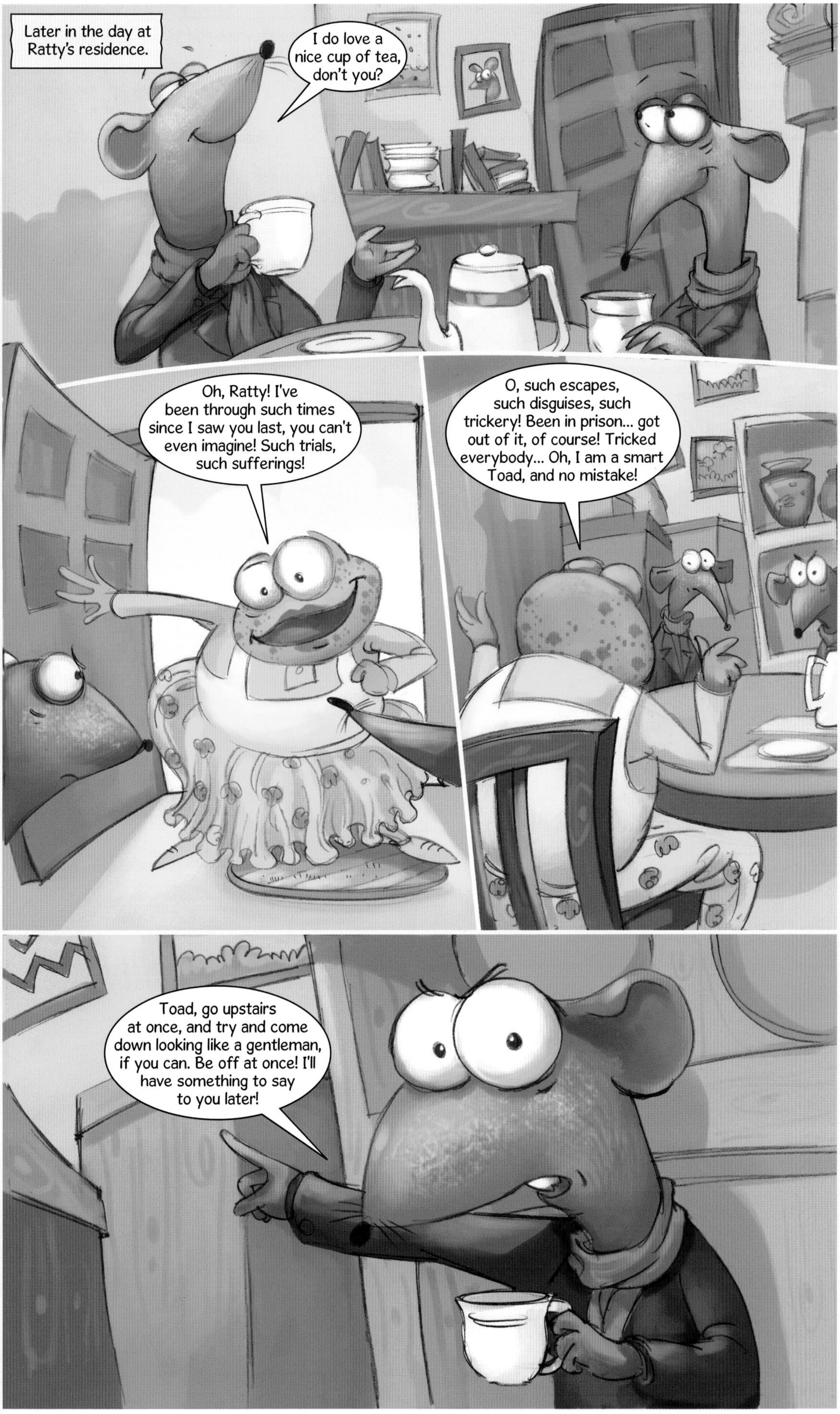
Later in the day at Ratty's residence.
I do love a nice cup of tea, don't you?
Oh, Ratty! I've been through such times since I saw you last, you can't even imagine! Such trials, such sufferings!
O, such escapes, such disguises, such trickery! Been in prison... got out of it, of course! Tricked everybody... Oh, I am a smart Toad, and no mistake!
Toad, go upstairs at once, and try and come down looking like a gentleman, if you can. Be off at once! I'll have something to say to you later!

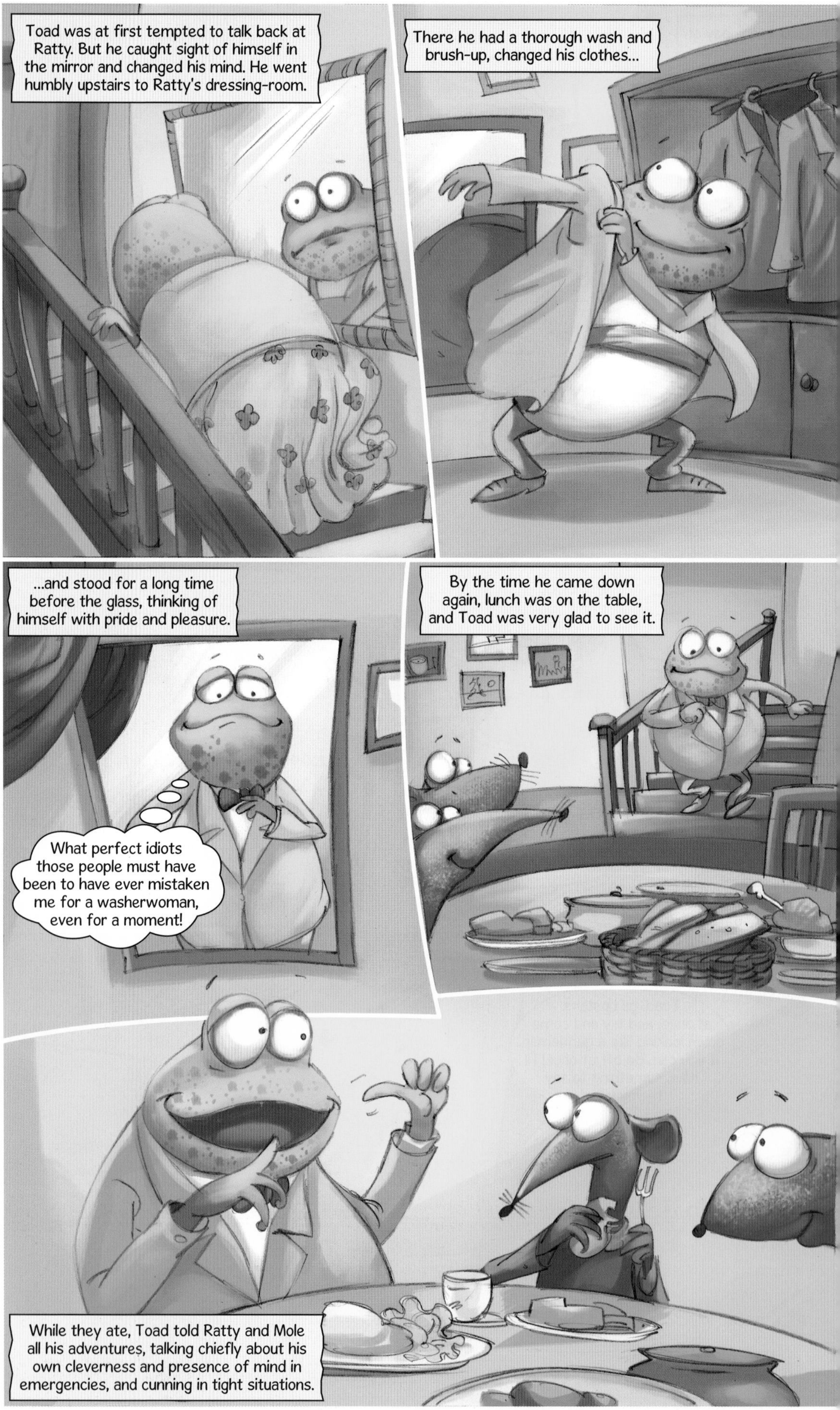
Toad was at first tempted to talk back at Ratty. But he caught sight of himself in the mirror and changed his mind. He went humbly upstairs to Ratty's dressing-room.
There he had a thorough wash and brush-up, changed his clothes...
...and stood for a long time before the glass, thinking of himself with pride and pleasure.
What perfect idiots those people must have been to have ever mistaken me for a washerwoman, even for a moment!
By the time he came down again, lunch was on the table, and Toad was very glad to see it.
While they ate, Toad told Ratty and Mole all his adventures, talking chiefly about his own cleverness and presence of mind in emergencies, and cunning in tight situations.

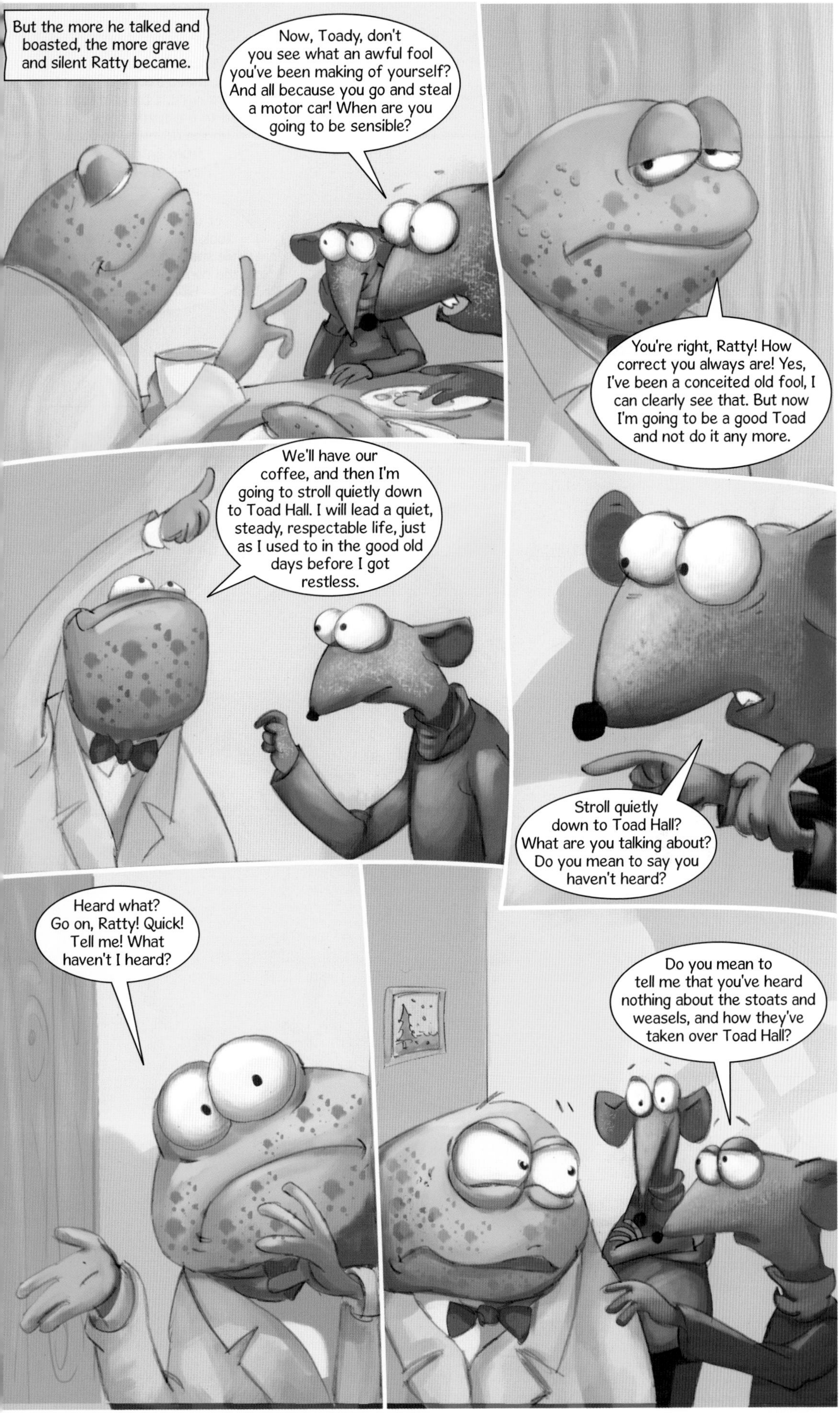
But the more he talked and boasted, the more grave and silent Ratty became.
Now, Toady, don't you see what an awful fool you've been making of yourself? And all because you go and steal a motor car! When are you going to be sensible?
You're right, Ratty! How correct you always are! Yes, I've been a conceited old fool, I can clearly see that. But now I'm going to be a good Toad and not do it any more.
We'll have our coffee, and then I'm going to stroll quietly down to Toad Hall. I will lead a quiet, steady, respectable life, just as I used to in the good old days before I got restless.
Stroll quietly down to Toad Hall? What are you talking about? Do you mean to say you haven't heard?
Heard what? Go on, Ratty! Quick! Tell me! What haven't I heard?
Do you mean to tell me that you've heard nothing about the stoats and weasels, and how they've taken over Toad Hall?

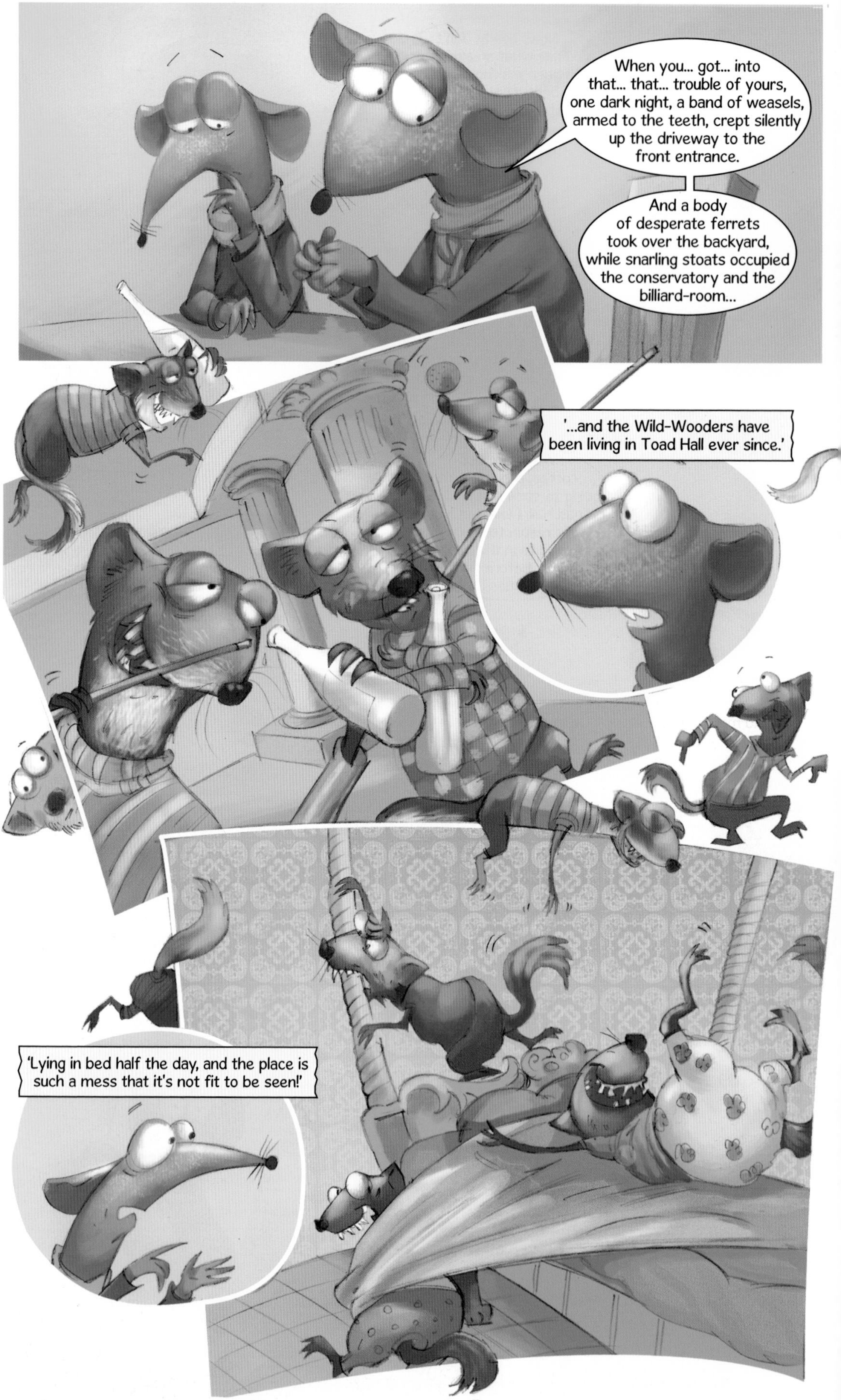

When you... got... into that... that... trouble of yours, one dark night, a band of weasels, armed to the teeth, crept silently up the driveway to the front entrance.
And a body of desperate ferrets took over the backyard, while snarling stoats occupied the conservatory and the billiard-room...
'...and the Wild-Wooders have been living in Toad Hall ever since.'
'Lying in bed half the day, and the place is such a mess that it's not fit to be seen!'

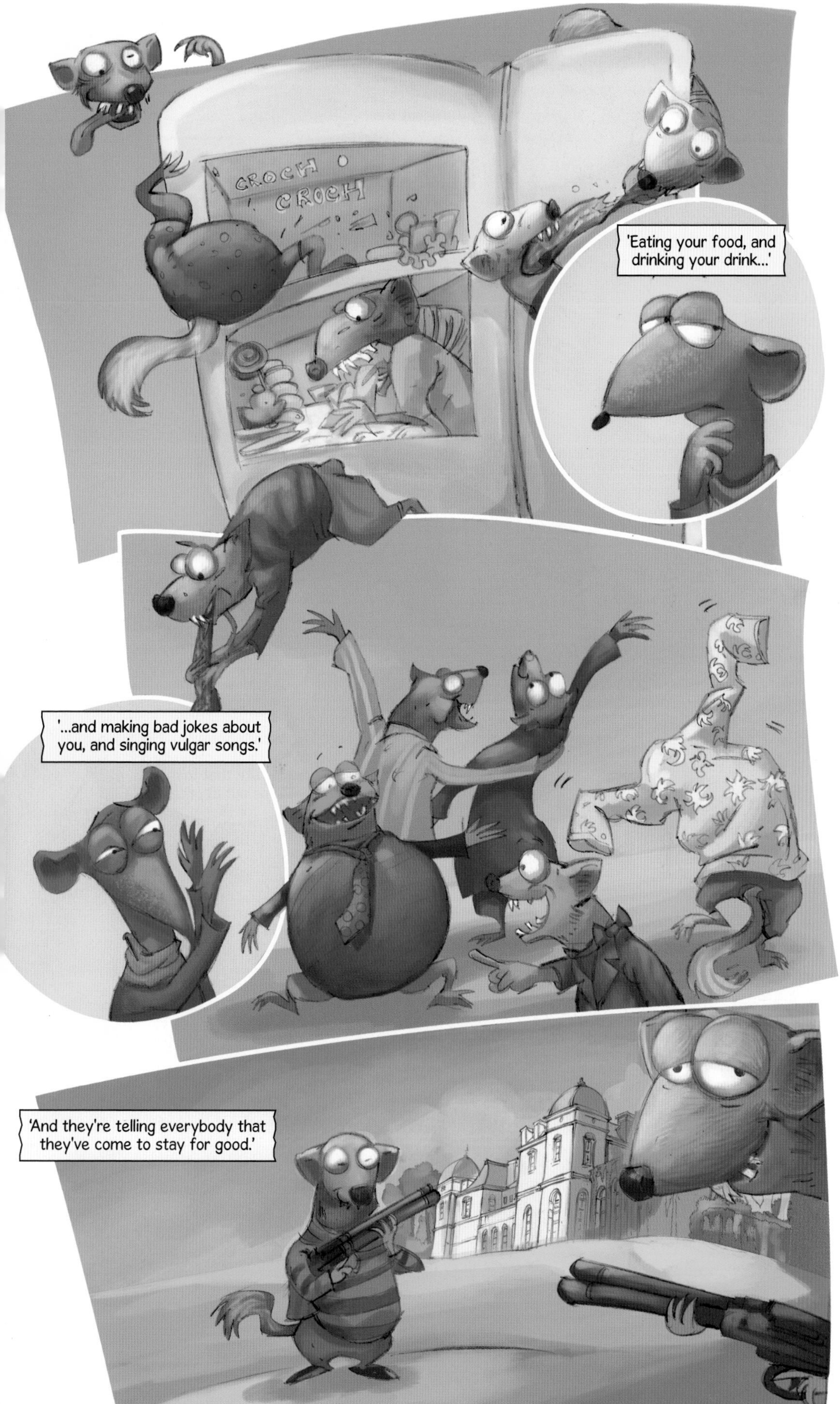
CROCH
CROCH
'Eating your food, and drinking your drink...'
'...and making bad jokes about you, and singing vulgar songs.'
'And they're telling everybody that they've come to stay for good.'

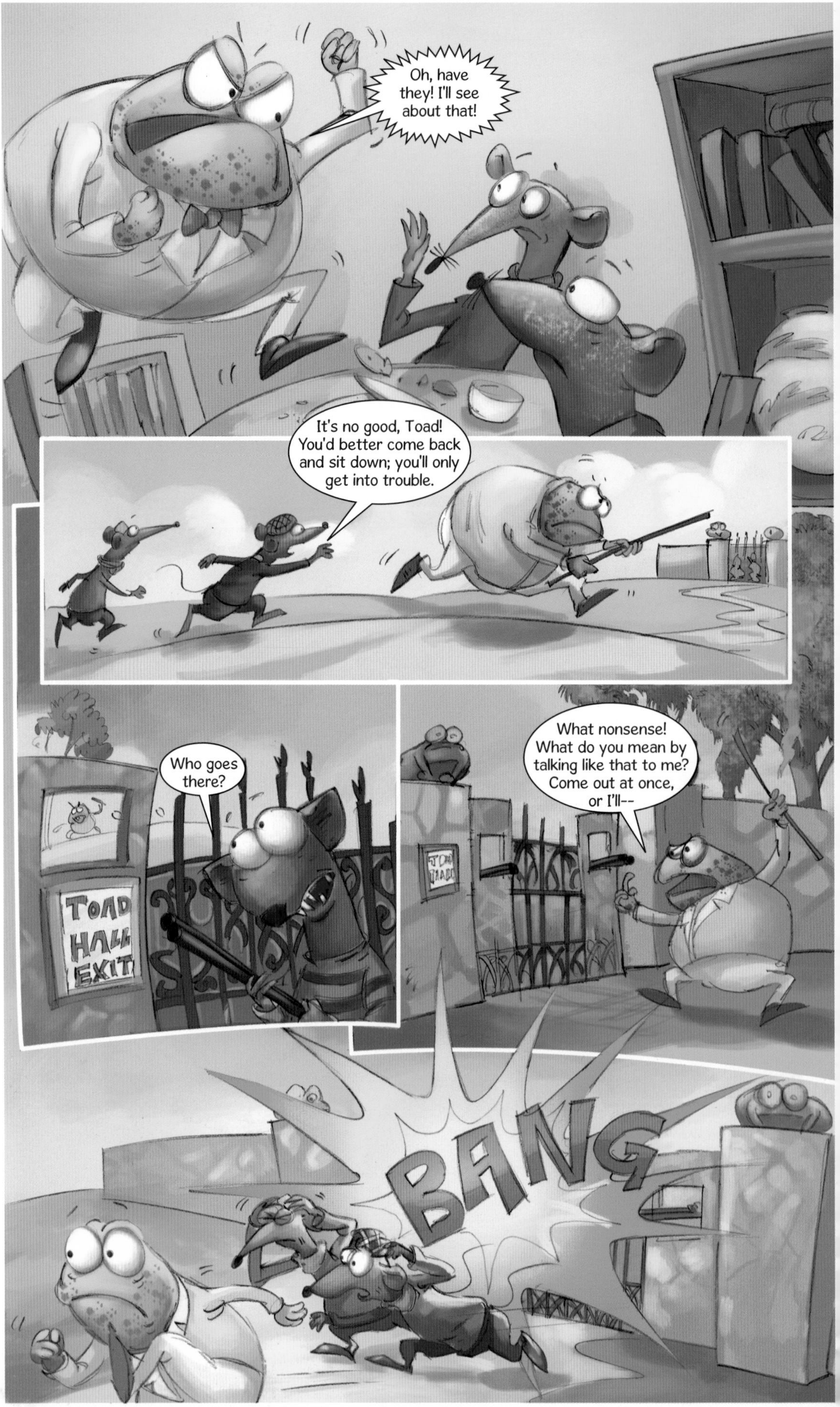

Oh, have they! I'll see about that!
It's no good, Toad! You'd better come back and sit down; you'll only get into trouble.
Who goes there?
TOAD HALL EXIT
What nonsense! What do you mean by talking like that to me? Come out at once, or I'll--
BANG

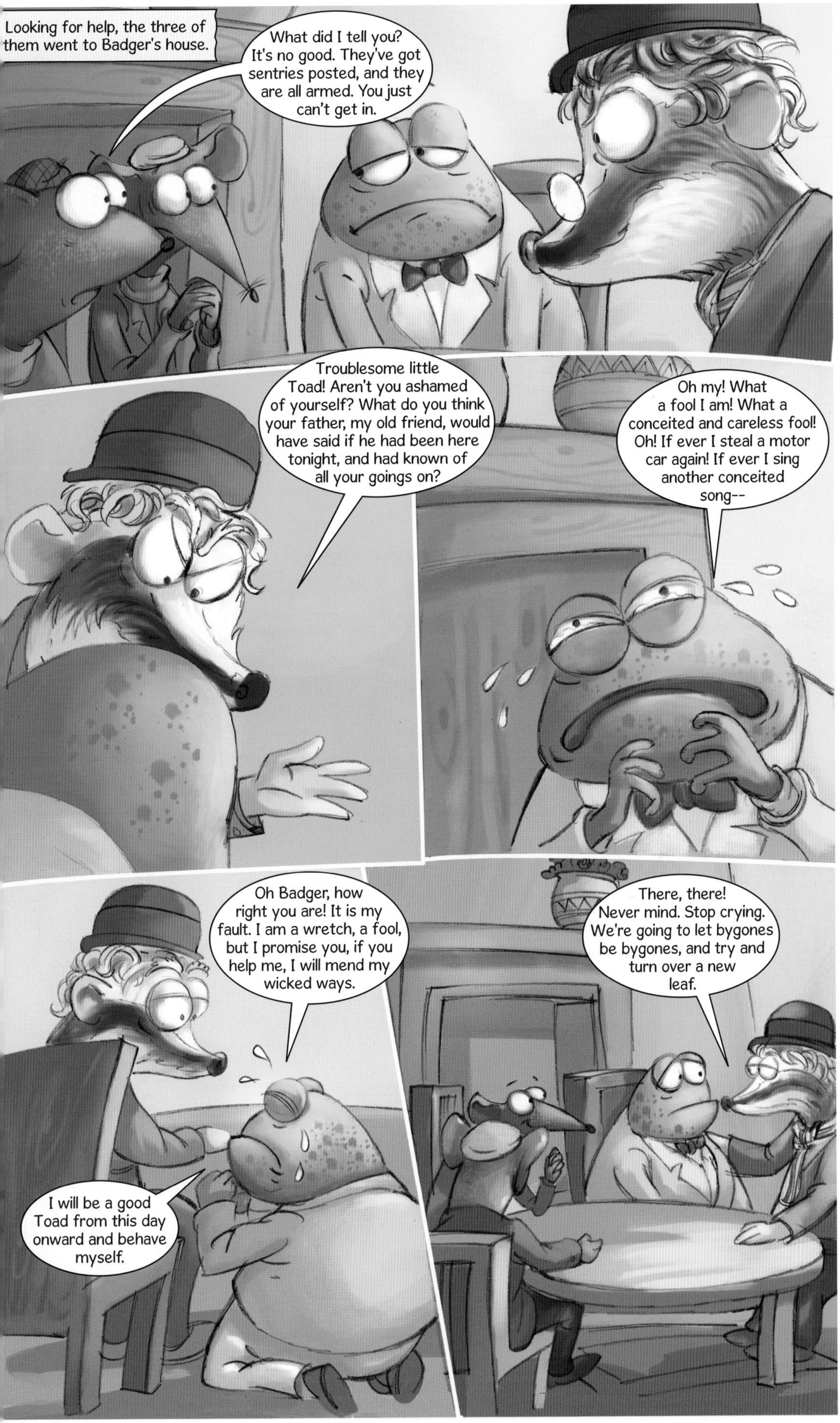
Looking for help, the three of them went to Badger's house.
What did I tell you? It's no good. They've got sentries posted, and they are all armed. You just can't get in.
Troublesome little Toad! Aren't you ashamed of yourself? What do you think your father, my old friend, would have said if he had been here tonight, and had known of all your goings on?
Oh my! What a fool I am! What a conceited and careless fool! Oh! If ever I steal a motor car again! If ever I sing another conceited song--
Oh Badger, how right you are! It is my fault. I am a wretch, a fool, but I promise you, if you help me, I will mend my wicked ways.
I will be a good Toad from this day onward and behave myself.
There, there! Never mind. Stop crying. We're going to let bygones be bygones, and try and turn over a new leaf.

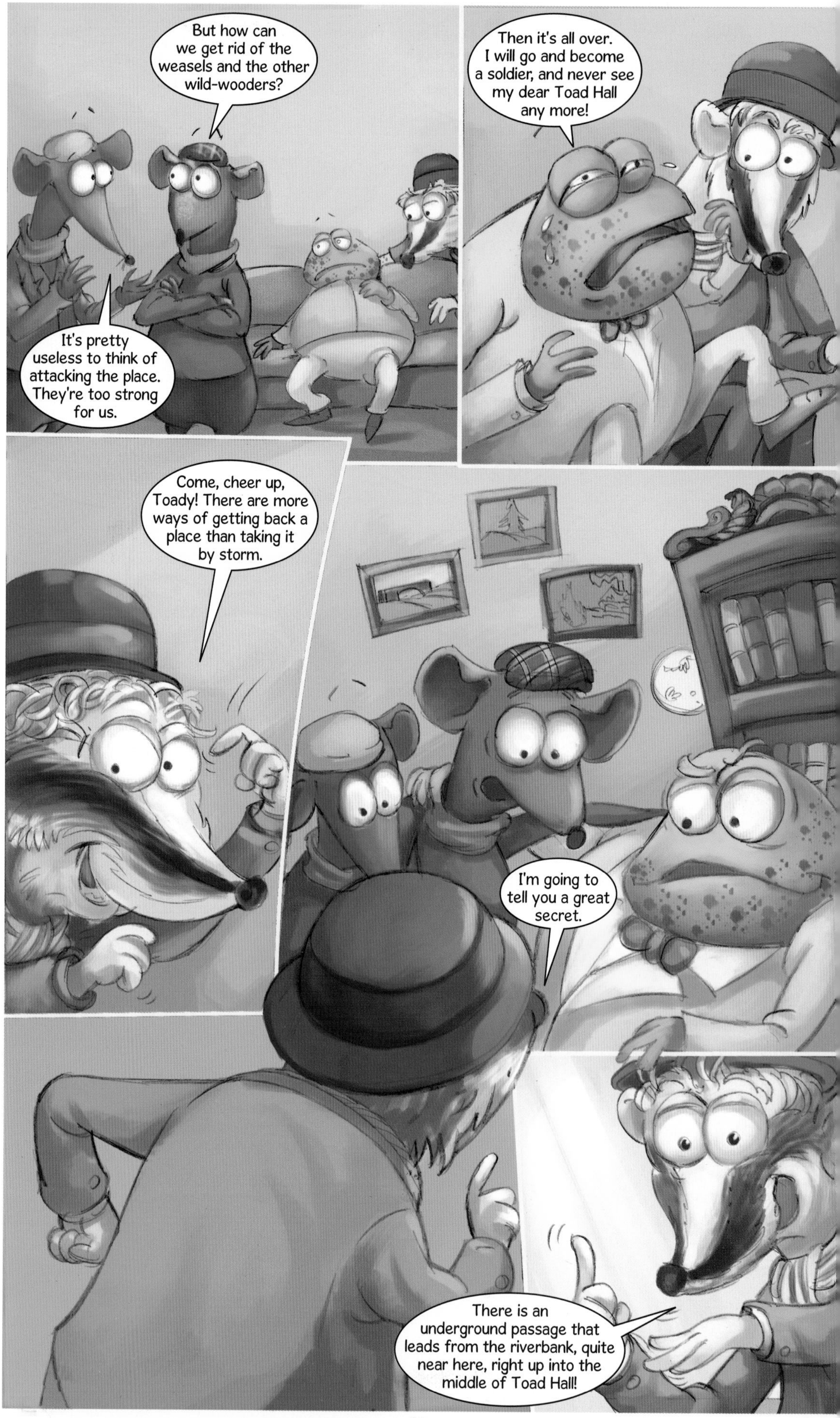
But how can we get rid of the weasels and the other wild-wooders?
It's pretty useless to think of attacking the place. They're too strong for us.
Then it's all over. I will go and become a soldier, and never see my dear Toad Hall any more!
Come, cheer up, Toady! There are more ways of getting back a place than taking it by storm.
I'm going to tell you a great secret.
There is an underground passage that leads from the riverbank, quite near here, right up into the middle of Toad Hall!

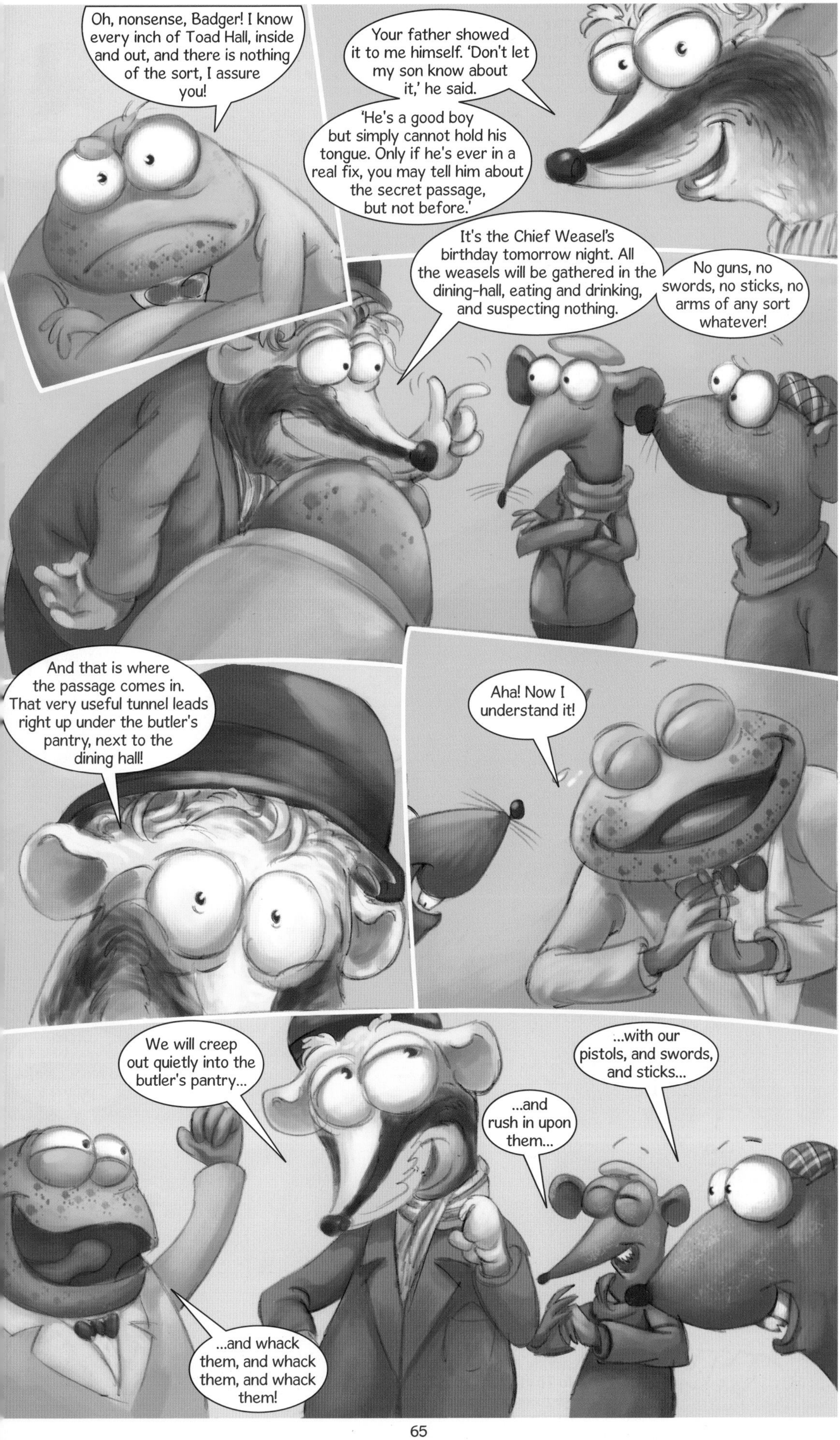
Oh, nonsense, Badger! I know every inch of Toad Hall, inside and out, and there is nothing of the sort, I assure you!
Your father showed it to me himself. 'Don't let my son know about it,' he said.
'He's a good boy but simply cannot hold his tongue. Only if he's ever in a real fix, you may tell him about the secret passage, but not before.'
It's the Chief Weasel's birthday tomorrow night. All the weasels will be gathered in the dining-hall, eating and drinking, and suspecting nothing.
No guns, no swords, no sticks, no arms of any sort whatever!
And that is where the passage comes in. That very useful tunnel leads right up under the butler's pantry, next to the dining hall!
Aha! Now I understand it!
We will creep out quietly into the butler's pantry...
...with our pistols, and swords, and sticks...
...and rush in upon them...
...and whack them, and whack them, and whack them!

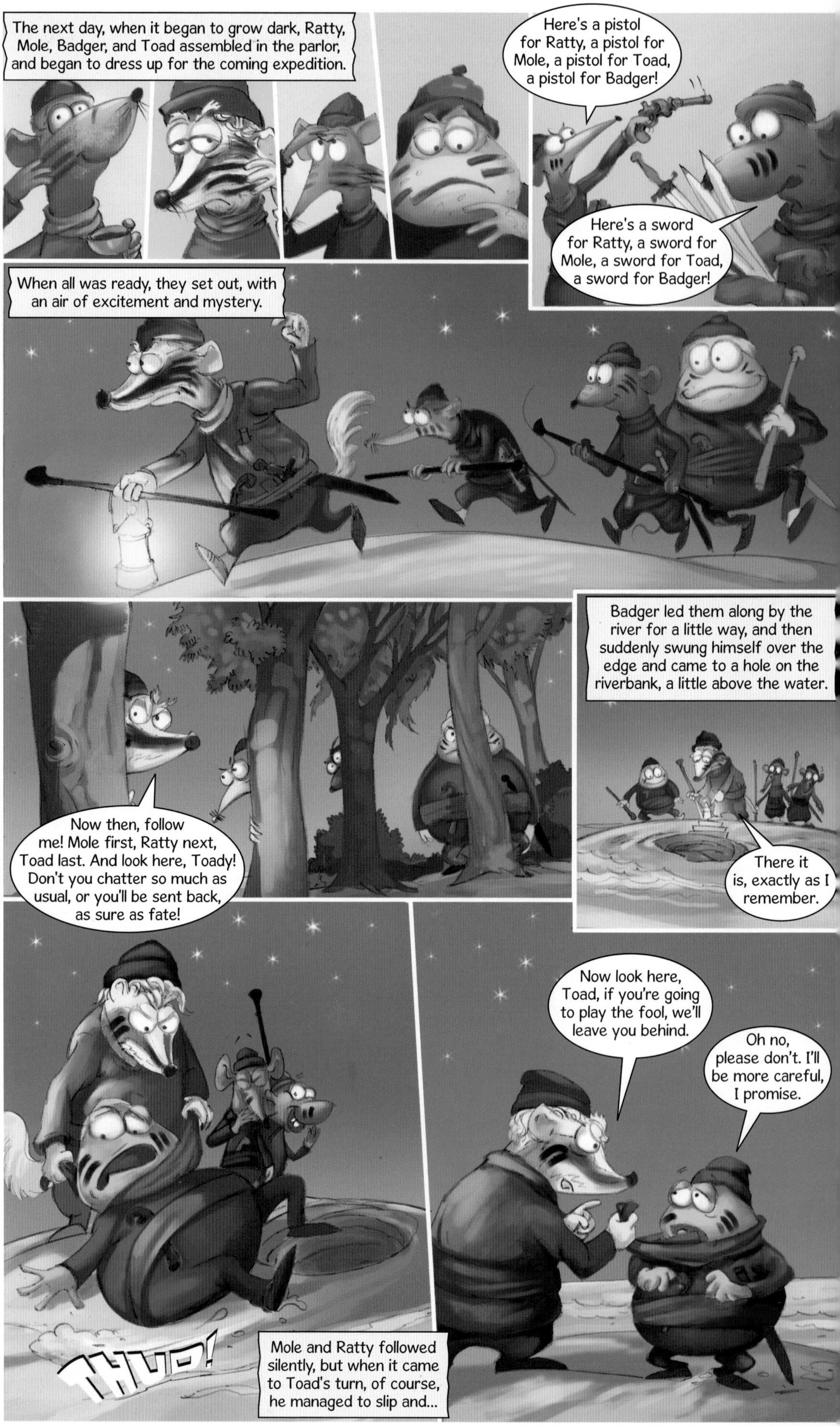

The next day, when it began to grow dark, Ratty, Mole, Badger, and Toad assembled in the parlor, and began to dress up for the coming expedition.
Here's a pistol for Ratty, a pistol for Mole, a pistol for Toad, a pistol for Badger!
Here's a sword for Ratty, a sword for Mole, a sword for Toad, a sword for Badger!
When all was ready, they set out, with an air of excitement and mystery.
Now then, follow me! Mole first, Ratty next, Toad last. And look here, Toady! Don't you chatter so much as usual, or you'll be sent back, as sure as fate!
Badger led them along by the river for a little way, and then suddenly swung himself over the edge and came to a hole on the riverbank, a little above the water.
There it is, exactly as I remember.
THUD!
Mole and Ratty followed silently, but when it came to Toad's turn, of course, he managed to slip and...
Now look here, Toad, if you're going to play the fool, we'll leave you behind.
Oh no, please don't. I'll be more careful, I promise.

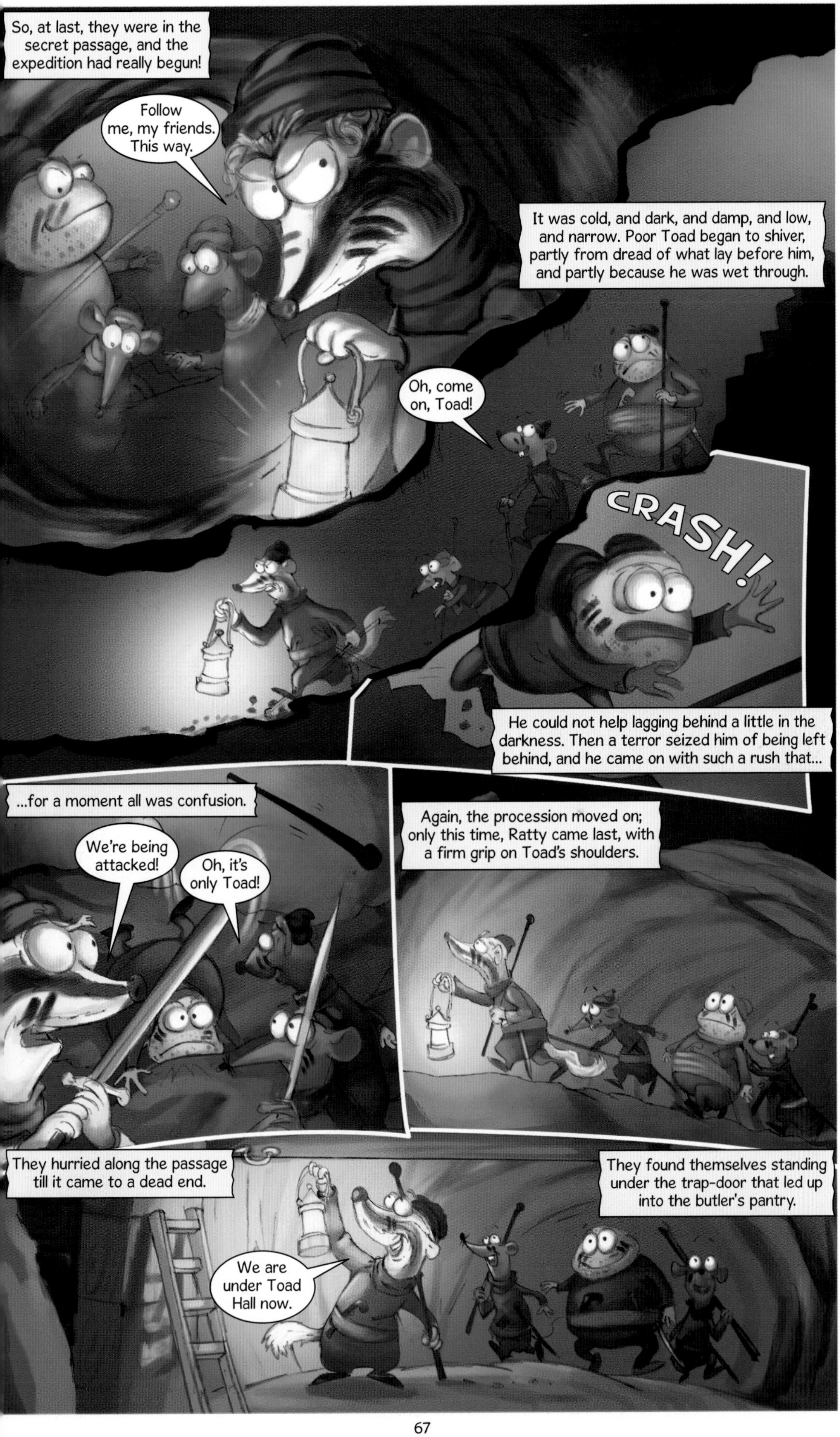
So, at last, they were in the secret passage, and the expedition had really begun!
Follow me, my friends. This way.
It was cold, and dark, and damp, and low, and narrow. Poor Toad began to shiver, partly from dread of what lay before him, and partly because he was wet through.
Oh, come on, Toad!
CRASH!
He could not help lagging behind a little in the darkness. Then a terror seized him of being left behind, and he came on with such a rush that...
...for a moment all was confusion.
We're being attacked!
Oh, it's only Toad!
Again, the procession moved on; only this time, Ratty came last, with a firm grip on Toad's shoulders.
They hurried along the passage till it came to a dead end.
They found themselves standing under the trap-door that led up into the butler's pantry.
We are under Toad Hall now.

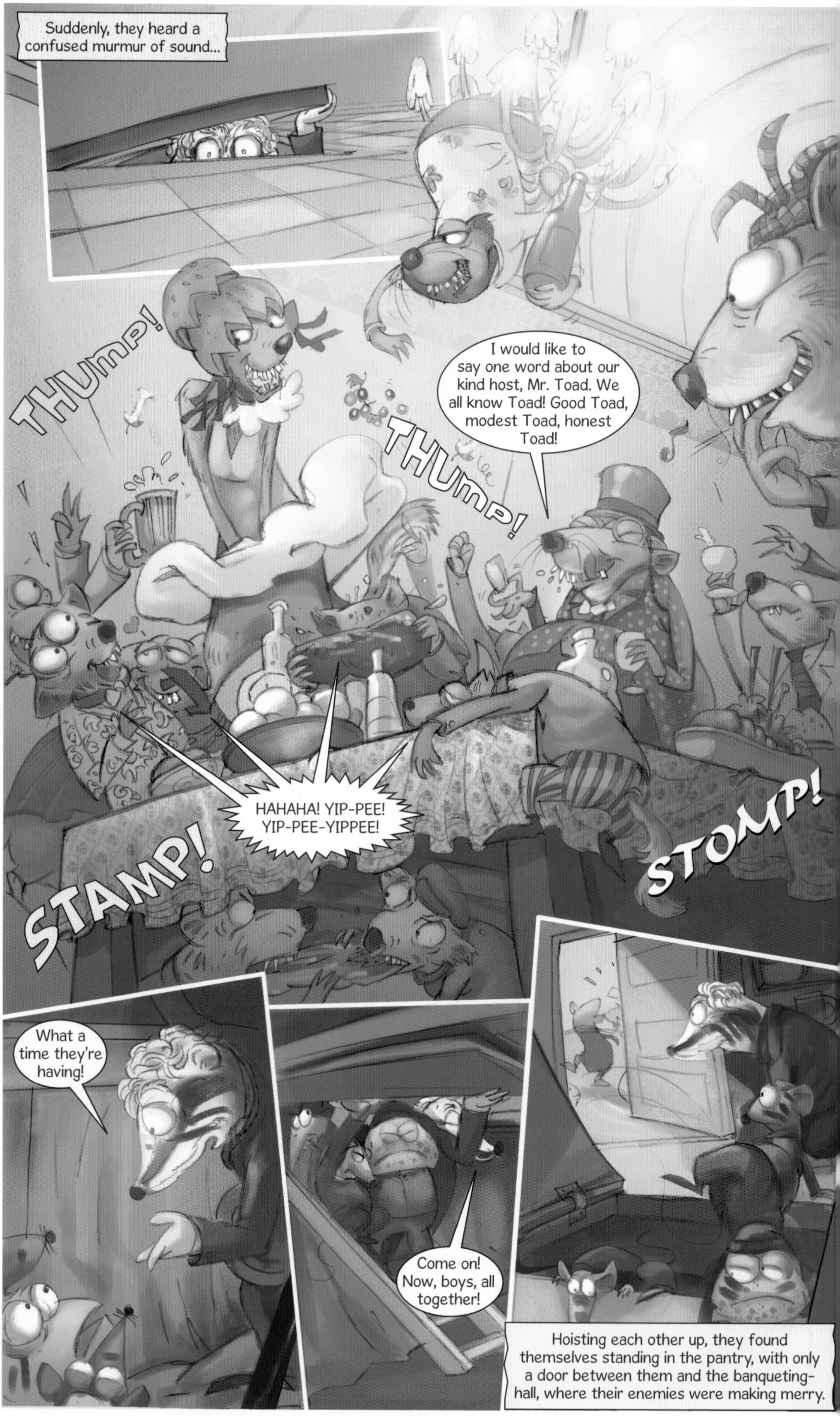

Suddenly, they heard a confused murmur of sound...
THUMP!
I would like to say one word about our kind host, Mr. Toad. We all know Toad! Good Toad, modest Toad, honest Toad!
THUMP!
HAHAHA! YIP-PEE! YIP-PEE-YIPPEE!
STAMP!
STOMP!
What a time they're having!
Come on! Now, boys, all together!
Hoisting each other up, they found themselves standing in the pantry, with only a door between them and the banqueting-hall, where their enemies were making merry.

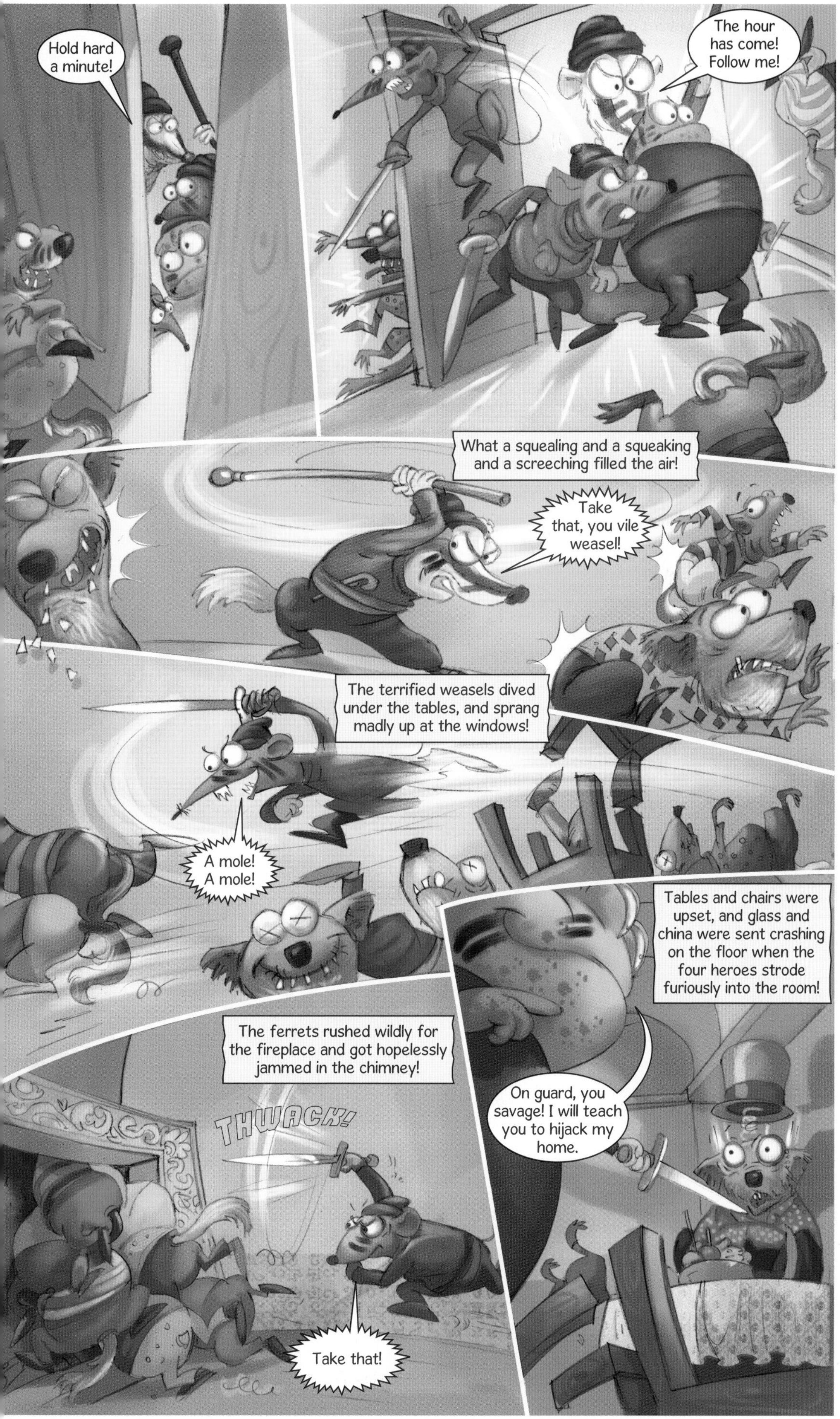
Hold hard a minute!
The hour has come! Follow me!
What a squealing and a squeaking and a screeching filled the air!
Take that, you vile weasel!
The terrified weasels dived under the tables, and sprang madly up at the windows!
A mole! A mole!
Tables and chairs were upset, and glass and china were sent crashing on the floor when the four heroes strode furiously into the room!
The ferrets rushed wildly for the fireplace and got hopelessly jammed in the chimney!
THWACK!
Take that!
On guard, you savage! I will teach you to hijack my home.

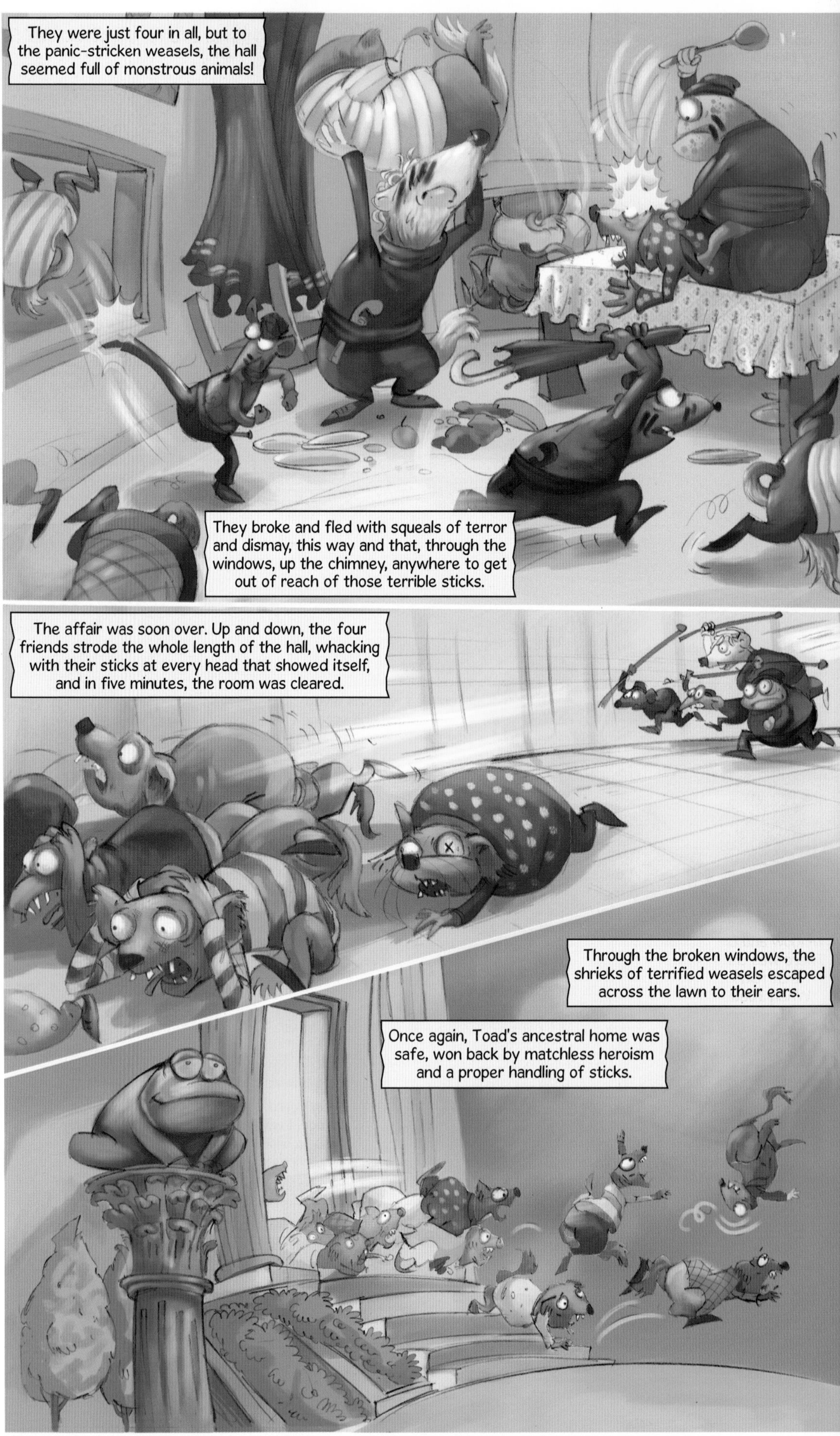
They were just four in all, but to the panic-stricken weasels, the hall seemed full of monstrous animals!
They broke and fled with squeals of terror and dismay, this way and that, through the windows, up the chimney, anywhere to get out of reach of those terrible sticks.
The affair was soon over. Up and down, the four friends strode the whole length of the hall, whacking with their sticks at every head that showed itself, and in five minutes, the room was cleared.
Through the broken windows, the shrieks of terrified weasels escaped across the lawn to their ears.
Once again, Toad's ancestral home was safe, won back by matchless heroism and a proper handling of sticks.

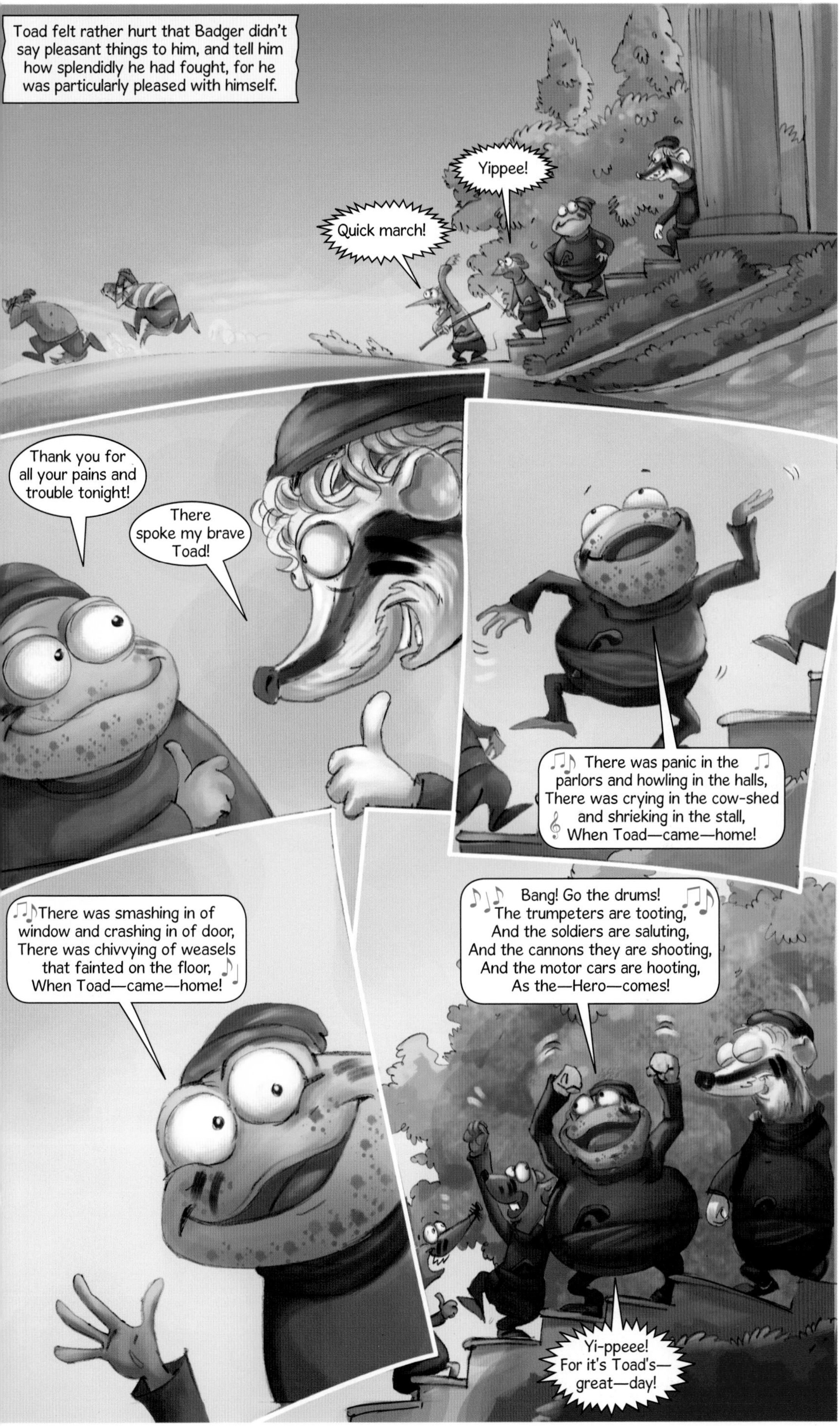
Toad felt rather hurt that Badger didn't say pleasant things to him, and tell him how splendidly he had fought, for he was particularly pleased with himself.
Yippee!
Quick march!
Thank you for all your pains and trouble tonight!
There spoke my brave Toad!
There was panic in the parlors and howling in the halls, There was crying in the cow-shed and shrieking in the stall, When Toad—came—home!
There was smashing in of window and crashing in of door, There was chivvying of weasels that fainted on the floor, When Toad—came—home!
Bang! Go the drums! The trumpeters are tooting, And the soldiers are saluting, And the cannons they are shooting, And the motor cars are hooting, As the—Hero—comes!
Yi-ppeee! For it's Toad's—great—day!

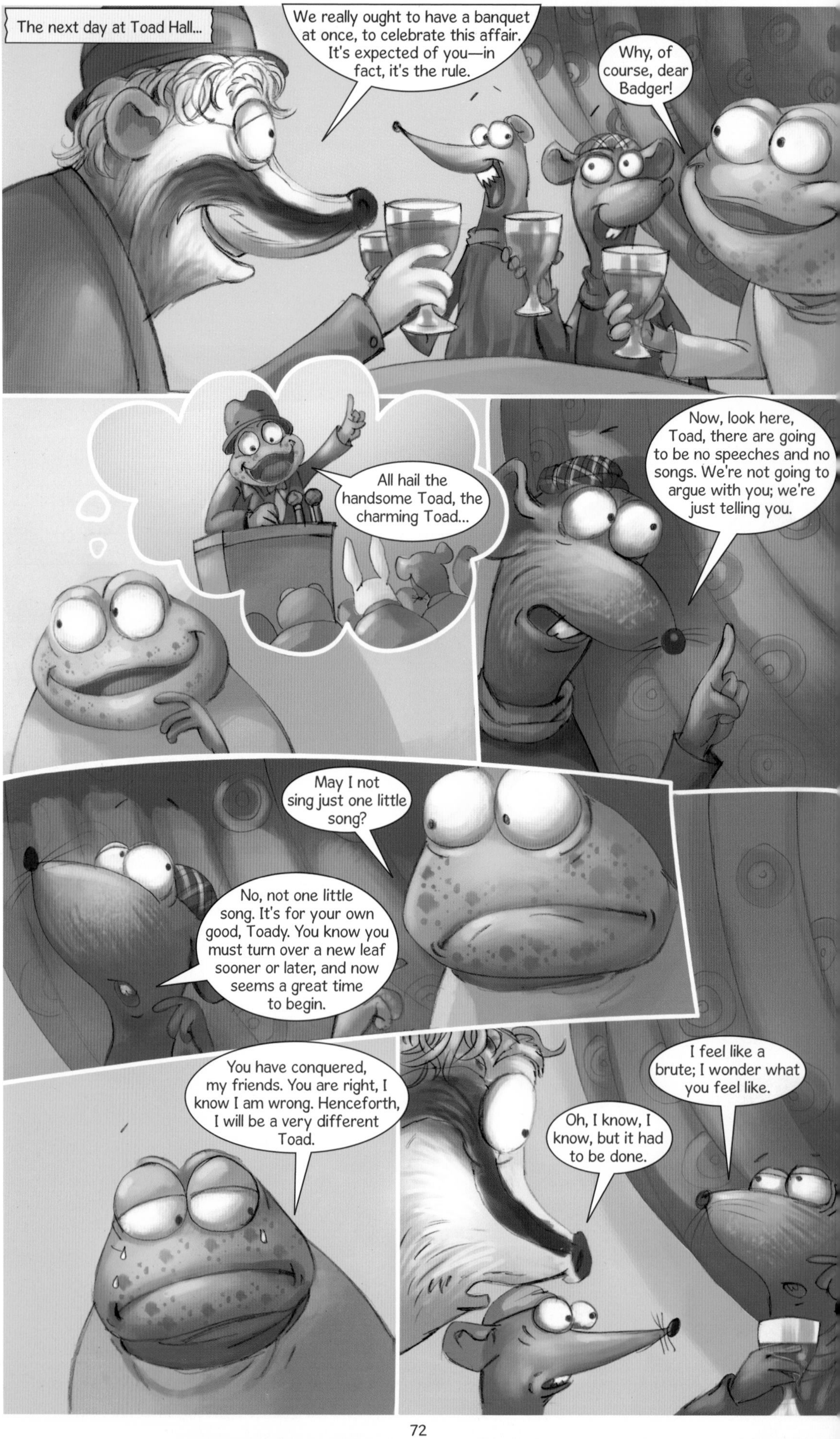

The next day at Toad Hall...
We really ought to have a banquet at once, to celebrate this affair. It's expected of you—in fact, it's the rule.
Why, of course, dear Badger!
All hail the handsome Toad, the charming Toad...
Now, look here, Toad, there are going to be no speeches and no songs. We're not going to argue with you; we're just telling you.
May I not sing just one little song?
No, not one little song. It's for your own good, Toady. You know you must turn over a new leaf sooner or later, and now seems a great time to begin.
You have conquered, my friends. You are right, I know I am wrong. Henceforth, I will be a very different Toad.
I feel like a brute; I wonder what you feel like.
Oh, I know, I know, but it had to be done.

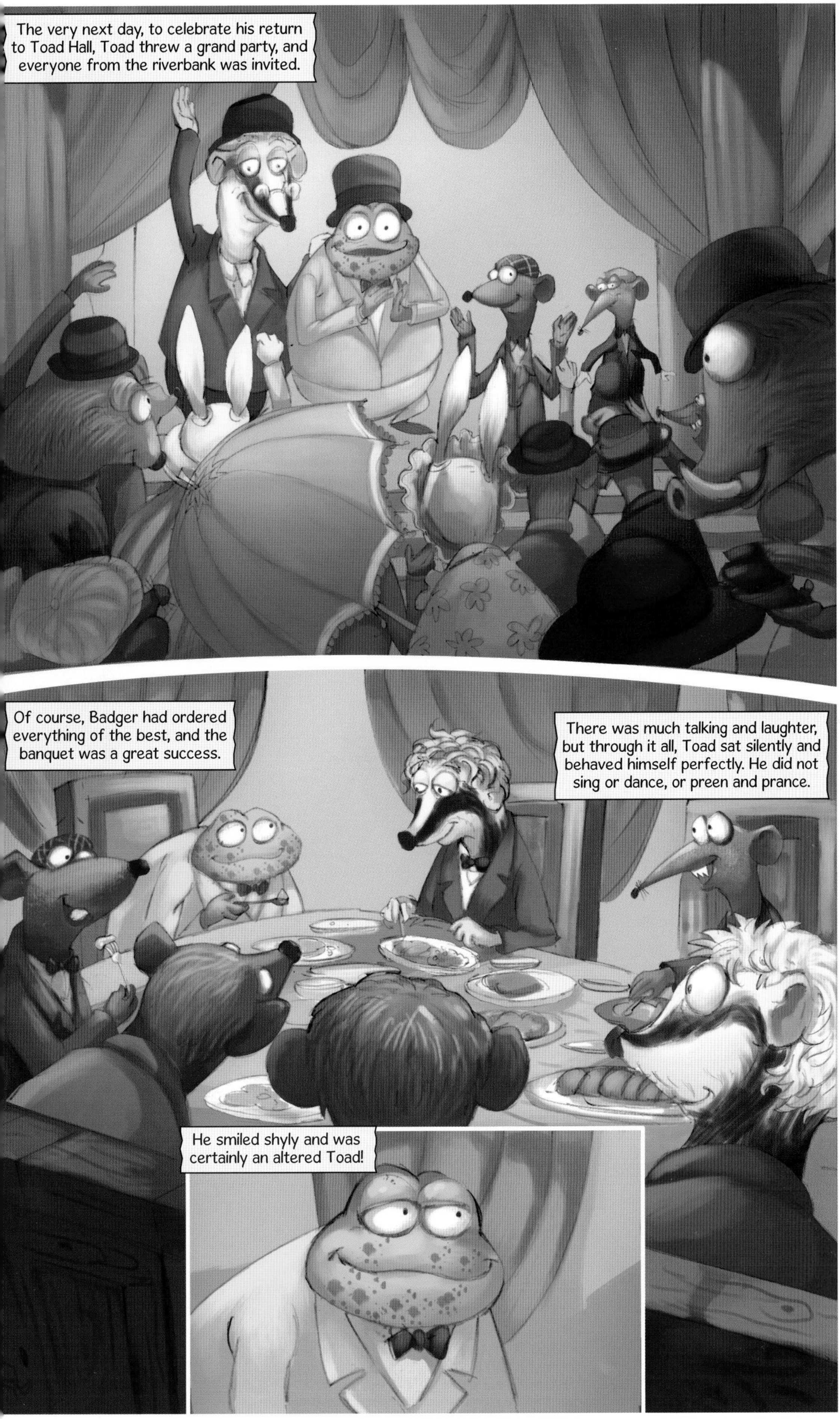
The very next day, to celebrate his return to Toad Hall, Toad threw a grand party, and everyone from the riverbank was invited.
Of course, Badger had ordered everything of the best, and the banquet was a great success.
There was much talking and laughter, but through it all, Toad sat silently and behaved himself perfectly. He did not sing or dance, or preen and prance.
He smiled shyly and was certainly an altered Toad!

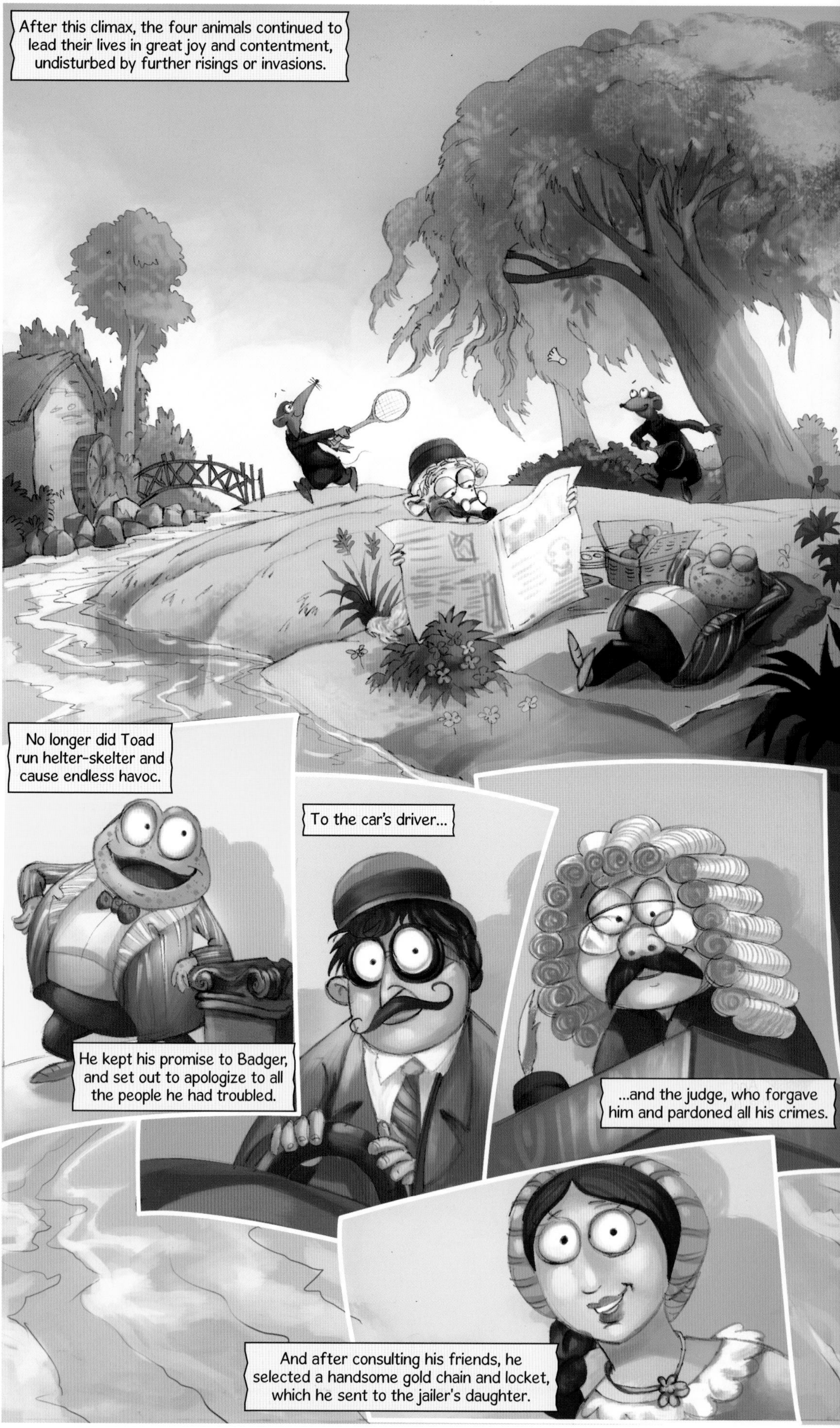
After this climax, the four animals continued to lead their lives in great joy and contentment, undisturbed by further risings or invasions.
No longer did Toad run helter-skelter and cause endless havoc.
He kept his promise to Badger, and set out to apologize to all the people he had troubled.
To the car's driver...
...and the judge, who forgave him and pardoned all his crimes.
And after consulting his friends, he selected a handsome gold chain and locket, which he sent to the jailer's daughter.

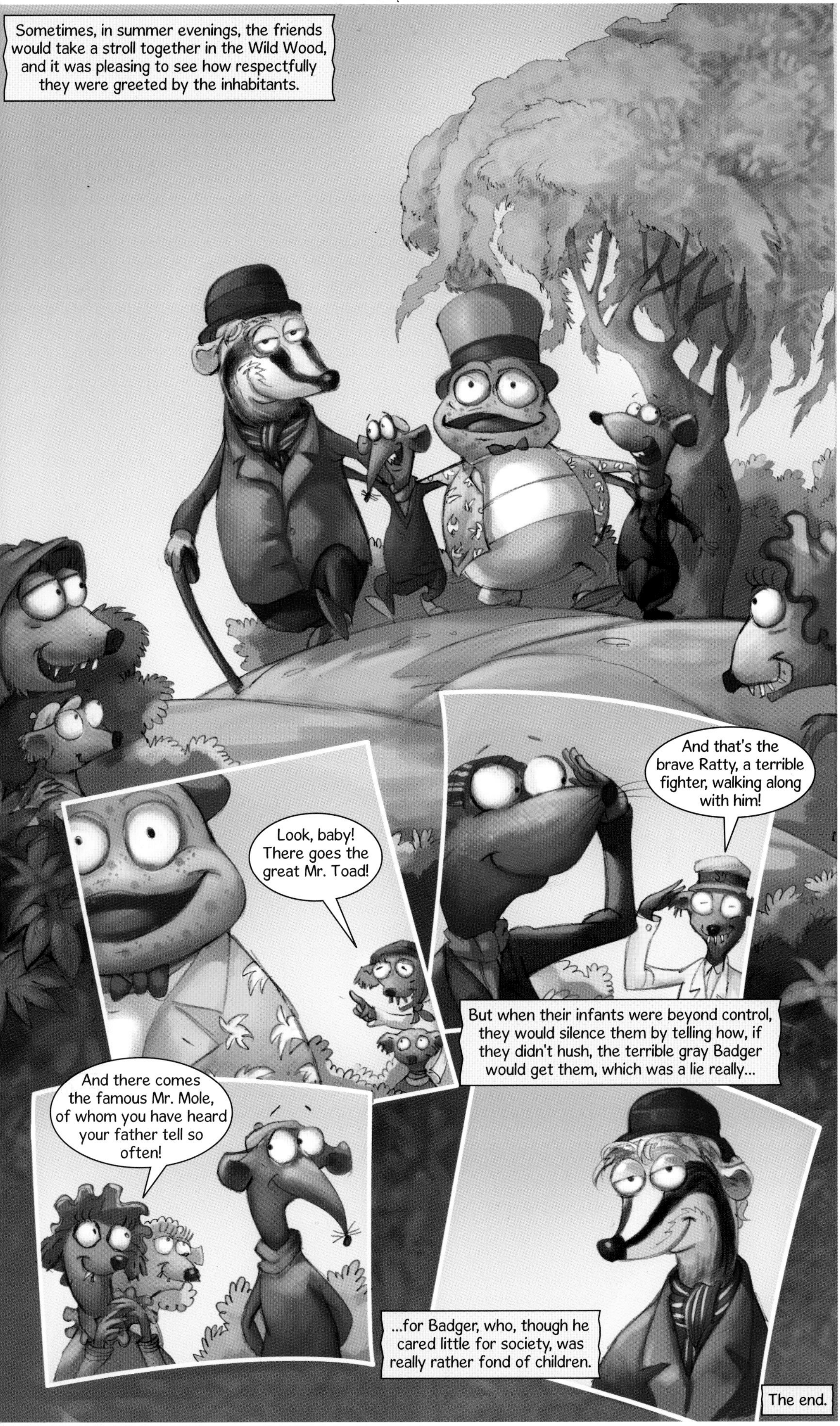
Sometimes, in summer evenings, the friends would take a stroll together in the Wild Wood, and it was pleasing to see how respectfully they were greeted by the inhabitants.
Look, baby! There goes the great Mr. Toad!
And that's the brave Ratty, a terrible fighter, walking along with him!
But when their infants were beyond control, they would silence them by telling how, if they didn't hush, the terrible gray Badger would get them, which was a lie really...
And there comes the famous Mr. Mole, of whom you have heard your father tell so often!
...for Badger, who, though he cared little for society, was really rather fond of children.
The end.

THE ENGLISH COUNTRYSIDE

The English countryside is blessed with beautiful wildlife. The variety of birds and animals found here are a treat to the eyes.

LONG-TAILED TIT

With its distinctive pink and white coloring, the Long-tailed Tit is an easily spotted bird of the English countryside. An amazing fact about these birds is their ability to construct a nest consisting of exactly 2,600 feathers, all of selected lengths to maintain the temperature of the nest for incubating and brooding young ones. When, for experimental purposes, the researchers tried increasing or decreasing the feathers, the birds readjusted the number accordingly!

BARN OWL

With a heart-shaped face, buff back and wings, and pure white under parts, the barn owl is a much loved English countryside bird. They have an effortless wavering flight that helps them to hunt silently, locating just by listening to the sound of the prey!

DID YOU KNOW?
An owl's eyes can only look forward in a fixed position and cannot move from side to side. In order to see peripherally, they move their head instead!

GOLDFINCH

Goldfinches are incredibly pretty birds with red faces and bright gold flashes along the edges of the wings. The goldfinch is the most popular and beautiful singing bird of the English countryside. It is also a great favorite among keepers of birds as pets. In the 19th century, goldfinches were favorite cage birds and were often trained to do tricks for the entertainment of visitors!

DID YOU KNOW?
Charm is the collective name for a group of goldfinches, because in olden times, it was considered to be a 'savior' bird and one that could ward off the plague!

WATER VOLES

These blunt-nosed, short-tailed rodents like to live in clean water in undisturbed riverbanks. They are regarded as inoffensive and harmless by the British, but Europeans consider them to be pests. Often mistaken for water rats, the water vole became 'Ratty' instead of 'Voley' in *The Wind in the Willows*!

BADGERS

Badgers are nature's own digging machines as they are capable of digging faster than a man can dig using a shovel! They dig long and complicated tunnels that end in a sleeping chamber. The badger regularly scratches its claws on a tree near its burrow to keep them in good condition for digging. Eurasian badgers often inhabit their burrows through generations.

DID YOU KNOW?
These heavy-set carnivores are known to be so aggressive that when they bite people, they don't let go until they hear the bones crack!

COMMON TOAD

If you see a frog walking rather than hopping in your garden, you should know that it is a toad and not a frog. The common toad has a natural inclination to walk, and is a familiar sight along waterways, parks, and gardens. Amazingly, they return to the same preferred ponds, year after year, passing by other, equally suitable, water bodies.

DID YOU KNOW?
The toad blinks to gulp its food. As they eat, the bulgy eyes close to help push the food down the toad's throat!

MOLE

The mole builds vast underground tunnels—always in two levels—in search of worms, insects, and nesting/living space. They can extend these tunnels at the rate of 100 feet per day! Often considered agricultural and lawn pests, they can at the same time benefit soil fertility by aerating and tilling it.

DID YOU KNOW?
Moles have large appetites and may eat up to 100 percent of their body weight in one day!

A - MAZED?

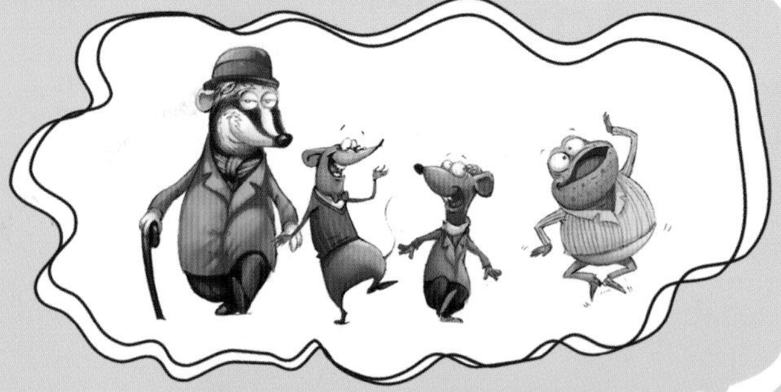

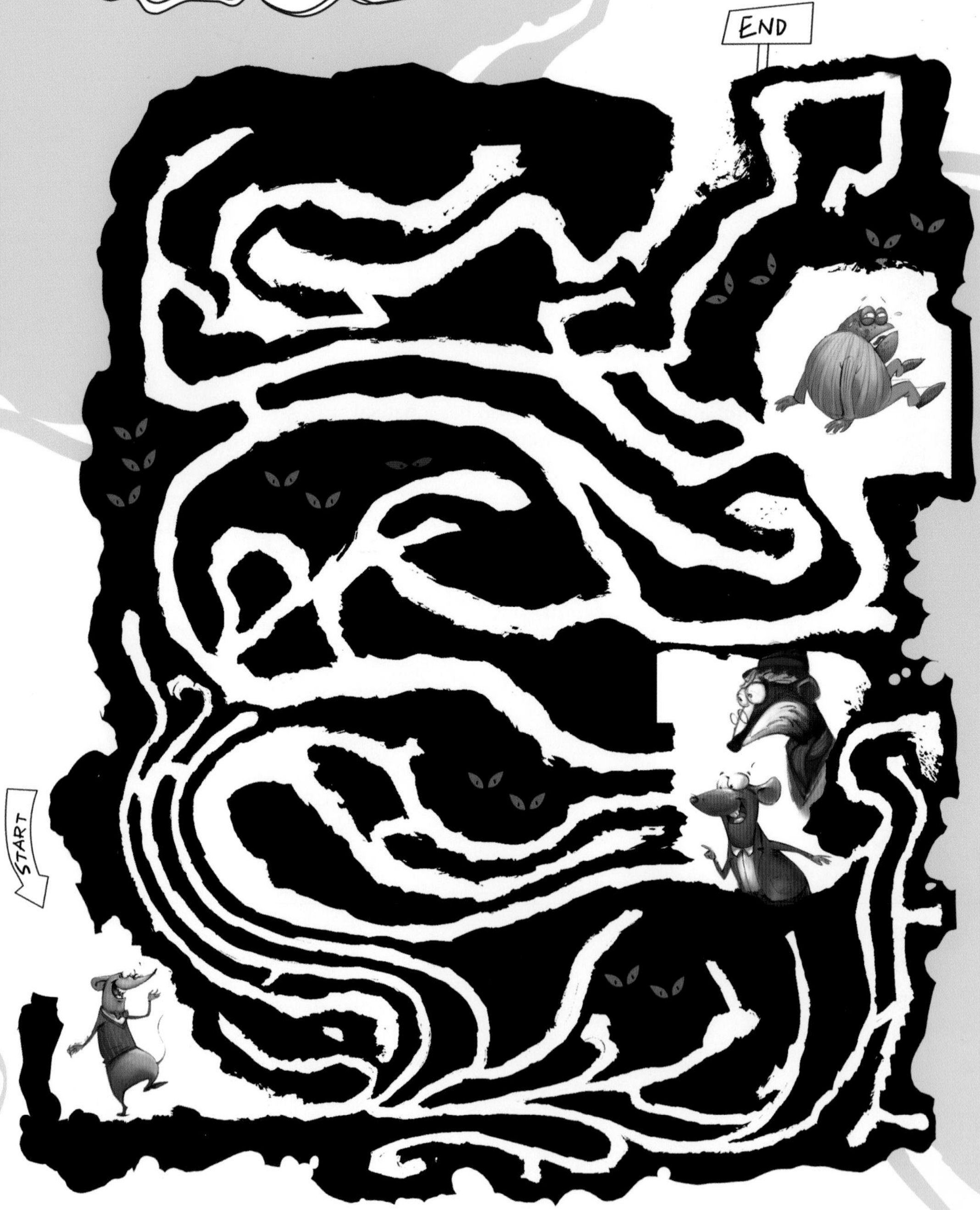
END
START

Toad is lost in a deep underground tunnel. Out to search for him, Badger and Ratty too lose their way. Can you help Mole find Badger and Ratty, and then rescue Toad?

WORD IT!

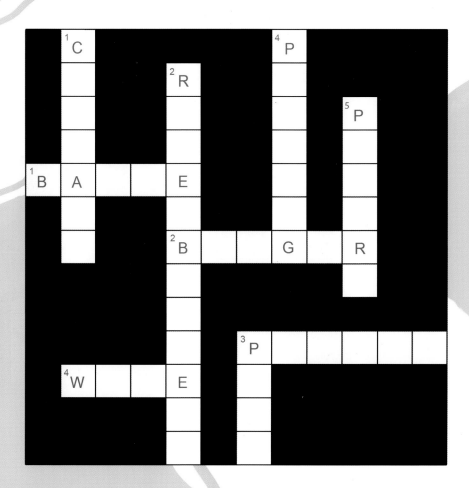

Down:
1. What Badger hates
2. What Ratty and Otter are called
3. What Toad says whenever he sees a motor car
4. One of toad's previous passions
5. The secret tunnel ended under the _________ of Toad Hall

Across:
1. A big boat carrying goods across the river
2. His name also means 'to pester'
3. Mole and Ratty have a ___________ on the river bank
4. ___________ World lies beyond the Wild Wood

Answers
Down:
1. Company 2. River bankers 3. Poop 4. Punting 5. Pantry
Across:
1. Barge 2. Badger 3.Picnic 4. Wide

Available now

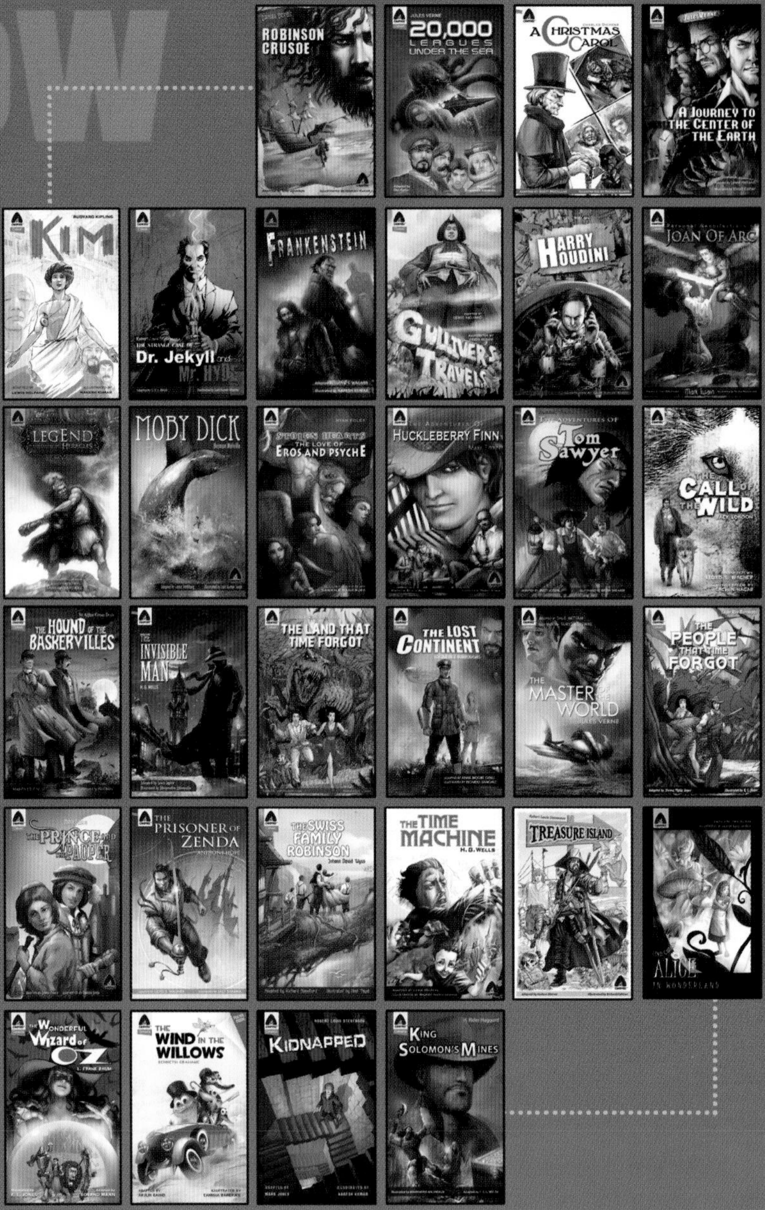
ROBINSON CRUSOE
JULES VERNE
20,000 LEAGUES UNDER THE SEA
A CHRISTMAS CAROL
A JOURNEY TO THE CENTER OF THE EARTH
RUDYARD KIPLING
KIM
THE STRANGE CASE OF Dr. Jekyll and Mr. Hyde
FRANKENSTEIN
GULLIVER'S TRAVELS
HARRY HOUDINI
JOAN OF ARC
LEGEND
MOBY DICK
EROS AND PSYCHE
HUCKLEBERRY FINN
Tom Sawyer
THE CALL OF THE WILD
THE HOUND OF THE BASKERVILLES
THE INVISIBLE MAN
THE LAND THAT TIME FORGOT
THE LOST CONTINENT
THE MASTER OF THE WORLD
THE PEOPLE THAT TIME FORGOT
THE PRINCE AND THE PAUPER
THE PRISONER OF ZENDA
THE SWISS FAMILY ROBINSON
THE TIME MACHINE
H. G. WELLS
TREASURE ISLAND
ALICE IN WONDERLAND
THE WONDERFUL WIZARD OF OZ
THE WIND IN THE WILLOWS
KIDNAPPED
KING SOLOMON'S MINES

Putting the fun back into reading!

Explore the latest from Campfire at

www.campfire.co.in